I0708166

Vespertine Dreams

Aster Rye

Copyright ©2023 Kami King Larsen

All rights reserved

Paperback ISBN: 979-8-9877140-1-0
Lily Fern Books

Cover Design: Brian Larsen
Cover photo and art: Kami Larsen

This is a work of fiction. Names, characters, places, and incidents are the products of the author's imagination or are used fictitiously and any resemblance to persons living or dead are coincidence.

3

For All of You

The King and the Knight

ONCE upon a time, there was a dashing king who lived in a palace built of words and stories rather than bricks and mortar. Where other palaces had buttresses and beams, this king's palace had ink and paper. In place of wood and glass, his palace had leather and canvas, glue and bindings, spines and parchment.

In each nook and cranny of the palace, stories lived and the dashing king was the keeper of them all. Plots were his servants, themes and tropes his court. Some of the pages told stories bold and daring others sweet yet intoxicating. Others still, clever, dull, or captivating. The monarch, like any just ruler, took care of them all, and while he had his favorites, each book and volume were treated as if it alone ruled his heart.

One day, while the young king was holding court, a dark wizard arrived and asked the king to kill a portion of his court and destroy a wing of his castle. The sorcerer argued these stories were too daring, too insightful, and too wonderful to be allowed to stay with the others. They would lead others astray he claimed. Only stories the sorcerer favored should be allowed to remain.

The king was appalled by this notion and told the sorcerer as much, but the evil wizard laughed at the king *calling him a weak ruler. The dark wizard offered to rule in his place, but only if the monarch would also banish the one person the king loved most in the world, his young son and heir to his throne.*

As the king loved the books equally—and the tiny prince even more—he refused and exiled the sorcerer from his realm, asking him to leave and never return. This of course angered the evil man and in a fit of rage, he set fire to the palace and all within its walls.

Unable to flee the burning embers, the dashing king was trapped in the palace. Thankfully, the young prince had been away from the castle on an adventure the day of the conflagration and was spared from the flames. The stories too, survived. They had a will of their own and could not be contained.

What happened next confused and surprised not only the king but the wizard as well. The wizard and the king were chained by the curse—bound to the palace of stories as well as each other.

1

TOURIST season was in full swing. It wasn't the families milling along the walkways and cobbled lanes, children enjoying shaved ice and parents applying sunscreen, which bothered Doria. Nor was it the groups of older ladies enjoying a weekend antiquing. It wasn't the solitary shoppers or the groups of high school students out for educational field trips. It was the happy couples—sun-kissed and holding hands—that drew her up short and made her curse the crowds. What right did they have to be enjoying the cool breeze and chittering birdsong while Miles could not? How could they steal kisses and looks of newly minted love when she was deprived of even a simple glimpse of Miles? How was it fair that they could stroll so casually in and out of shops and boutiques when the only door to the only shop *she* wanted to visit was lost to her?

It had been weeks since Doria shared what was arguably the most memorable night of her life in the arms of the man who had managed to break through her barriers and reel her into a mystery so vast and unexpected. When she'd walked out the door of Vespertine Books that night, she knew she would do anything to help Miles break the curse that chained him to the wonderous shop. What she didn't know, was that the shop itself would be lost to her, and in turn, so would Miles.

Every evening since that night, she'd returned only to find blank walls and graffiti covered alleyways. No worn wooden sign. No glass inset door. No Miles.

Cassie and Elenor had told Doria the shop could do that— not disappear per se, but cloak itself, making the entrance impossible to find. They had all believed Doria's connection to Miles would keep such a thing from happening. They'd all just assumed, the door would appear as it generally did and offer admittance to Doria when she wanted to visit. They'd all been wrong.

So once again, Doria fought the crowded streets and waded through the throngs of tourists and locals alike. She scanned each road and studied each alcove. Not just the spaces between the used appliance store and the consignment boutique where the entrance generally liked to pop up, but along each strip mall and business district in town. It was no use. Vespertine Books might as well have never existed for all the good her searching did.

It wasn't just that she yearned to see Miles again, although that did play a big part in her frustration. She also wanted to sit in the shop. Soak in the smell of the ink and paper. Run her hands over the bindings and spines. Snuggle into her favorite overstuffed chair and crack open a book that would take her away for just a few hours. Between her shifts at the café, meetings with Cassie and Elenor, research time spent trying to decipher the cryptic writing tattooed on Miles' arm, and looking into occult curses and local legends, Doria hadn't had any time to just sit with a good book and read an amazing story.

It was the stories that had gotten her entangled in all this to begin with. Her love for edge-of-your-seat thrillers and her disdain for romance and fluff fantasy had been what drew Miles to her in the first place. She missed sitting and talking to him about plots and tropes, characters and settings. She wanted to know what he would suggest to her next and wanted to know if she'd love it or loathe it. But none of that was going to happen unless she could find the damn door.

So, for the fifth time that night, she turned the corner by the grungy little bar and did what she did every night. She hoped.

The front door shutting jolted Doria from the thin sleep she was under. She sat up on the couch and tried to calm her pattering heart.

"Hey peaches," Felicity said. "Don't take this the wrong way, but I was hoping not to see you tonight. No luck, huh?"

Doria yawed and scrubbed her eyes with the heels of her hands. "Nope."

"How about Cassie?"

"She's tried three times this week and nothing. She says it's the longest stretch she's had without being able to get in." Miles' niece generally visited Vespertine Books at least three or four times per week. "Elenor's even tried and no luck."

Felicity dropped down beside her. "Look, I know you think this has something to do with you, but do not blame yourself for this."

"I'm trying not to, but you have to admit, it seems a tad bit coincidental that. . . well you know." Doria finished lamely.

"Coincidental that the night after you banged the hunky cursed book nerd, the shop closed up for good? That would be the worst ending to a great story ever." Doria's roommate bumped shoulders with her. "The sex couldn't have been that bad." She laughed.

"It definitely was not." Doria smiled. "Maybe it's part of the curse? I don't know. Miles seemed happy. Maybe whatever that little prick Peter Smith did had some kind of Buffy and Angel clause."

"I'm not following."

Doria huffed and shook her head. "You are so uncultured. You know—when Angel was finally happy after he and Buffy did the deed, he became a soulless vampire again? Maybe when Peter cursed Miles and the shop, there was some kind of trigger or something. It's the only thing I can think of."

"Oh my god. That is awful." Felicity squeezed Doria's shoulder. "Whatever it is, we will figure it out. Have you gotten anywhere with the tattoo?"

"No. It's another epic fail. I've looked online for every possible language I can think of. I've googled until my eyeballs are about to fall out and I can't find anything that resembles the characters. For all I know, it could be Peter's idea of a joke."

"Yikes. What time do you work tomorrow?"

"I've got the early shift."

"Any plans after?"

"More of the same."

"There's a used book sale tomorrow at the library. I saw the notice in my feed today. Let's hit it up. I'm sure there's some disturbing psycho-killer novel out there you haven't read yet. If we're in luck, maybe we can see if Cassie has had any luck with the tattoo. There's got to be someone out there who'll know what it is."

Doria nodded. "That sounds good." Maybe she was right. As a librarian, Cassie had to have better access to search functions and academic resources.

It wasn't a psycho killer novel she wanted though. It was a great fantasy romance she could devour and then discuss with Miles. She couldn't bring herself to tell Felicity that however. She knew if she tried she might break down and not be able to put herself back together.

The tables had been set out on the lawn in front of the library and dozens of patrons dug through the boxes and stacks for literary gems to take home. Doria couldn't blame them. For five dollars, they could fill a shopping bag with the treasures.

Doria scanned the titles. Many of the books were hardcovers in nearly new conditions. There was an abundance of police procedurals, espionage mysteries, and celebrity book club picks. She found a few titles from previous best-seller's lists and placed them in her bag alongside a slightly dog eared but complete trilogy of young adult horrors she'd been wanting to read for quite some time, and an intriguing collection of sci-fi shorts.

As she drifted over to a table at the end, she saw a pair of moms pushing strollers. They each had tote bags overflowing with paperbacks. One of the women, a petite woman in yoga pants with hair the color of sunshine, pointed at a book with a slightly worn dust jacket. The artwork on the cover was simple but beautiful.

"Have you read that one?" she asked the tired looking woman at her side.

"Of course," her friend replied. "People love that book. I love that book. Even my husband's mother loves that book. She's an amazing author."

"Top five on my list, her friend responded. The second one in the series is even better than the first."

Doria couldn't help herself. She reached over and picked it up. "You aren't buying this one then?"

"Oh, no honey. You go ahead. You haven't read it yet?" The mom with the golden ponytail asked.

"Nope. It's a newer genre for me," Doria explained as she looked at the jacket synopsis.

"You should definitely grab this one too then," the shorter of the moms said as she handed over a thinner volume by the same author. "These are her novellas. I always love the side character stories."

"Thanks." Doria smiled as she put the two books in her bag and left to find Felicity.

Six months ago, she would have avoided the romantasy table at all costs. But her reading habits were changing. She still loved a good grisly blood and guts kind of book, but Miles had slowly been convincing her of some of the joy that could be found in a well-written romantic fantasy. She didn't want to forget that joy, even if being separated from him made it feel distant and painful at times.

Maybe when she got home, she'd take just a few minutes for herself and dive into one of the books in her tote. Miles was probably reading wherever he was anyway. Not as if he had much else to do. Curling up with a book for even just a handful of minutes might make him feel closer in some way.

Felicity met her near the checkout table. "Do you have room for this in your bag? It's the only thing I could find." She handed over a pristine paperback. The spine didn't look as if it had ever been cracked. When Doria read the title—*101 Stories to Read in the John*—she just sighed and shook her head.

"What?" Fel asked.

"This is all you could find?"

Felicity grinned ear to ear. "You're the reader, not me."

Doria stopped at a folding table and handed the volunteer there a crumpled ten-dollar bill.

"Let me get you some change." The man smiled cheerfully at her as he dug into a battered bank bag.

"Please." Doria held up her hand in a stop gesture. "Keep it as a donation." She dipped her head toward her tote. "These are still quite a bargain at that price."

"Will do. You have a good day now." He handed her a flyer on bright orange paper, a large smiling jack o' lantern decorating the bottom. "Next sale is in three months. Make sure you stop by then too."

Doria stuffed the paper into her bag alongside the books.

They were just at the bottom of the library steps when she saw him. Peter Smith. He was standing across the small parking lot, partially hidden under the canopy of a large oak. The weasel was watching her.

As soon as she made eye contact with him, he turned and hurried away. Shoving the tote at her roommate, she took off after him.

"Peter. Wait," she called. "I just want to talk. Please."

He wasn't running, but he certainly wasn't slowing down either. "Peter!"

She stepped into the parking area; eyes focused solely on the retreating man. Tires squealed and the SUV came to a shuddering halt just in front of her. She'd never even noticed it backing out of the space. Thank god the driver was paying attention. Doria's eyes flew to the driver—the shorter mom she'd gotten the book recommendation from earlier. The woman had a hand on her chest, a panicked look in her eyes.

"Sorry," Doria cringed in apology.

The woman looked over her shoulder at the car seat fastened in behind her, then with a relieved look, waved Doria off.

By the time Doria looked back across the lot, Peter Smith had vanished. With a sigh of frustration, she retreated toward the library steps. Unable to pin down Peter, she made do with the hope that Cassie would be able to pull a miracle out of her computer.

Cassie had the kind of quiet beauty Doria envied. If she looked half as good at her age, Doria would be beyond thrilled. With a simple pixie haircut and minimalistic makeup, she radiated both good health and good genes.

"Hello lovely ladies," she said as the women approached the reference desk. "Any news worth me knowing about?"

"I just saw Peter Smith outside," Doria replied, but before Cassie could ask, she continued, "but he got away. I didn't even get a chance to punch him in the throat, much less ask what sort of wicked curse he put on the place."

Felicity stifled a laugh at her roommate's casual reference to violence, but Cassie continued to look stricken. "That is unfortunate. I feel at my wit's end."

"No hits then on the tattoo?" Felicity asked.

"I've looked through almost everything we have here and can't find a match. But honestly, it isn't really all that surprising.

We're a small-town public library, not an academic institution. But," she tilted her head and drew out the word. Doria felt a small bud of hope blossom in her chest. "I sent an email to one of my friends up at the university. She's been having an illicit affair with a professor in the linguistics department. It's all very inappropriate." She grinned devilishly.

"Cassie. You scoundrel. What did you do?" Felicity asked.

"Nothing much. Just mentioned that she owed me one for keeping my mouth shut. They could both be a bit of trouble if it got out. Anyway, she was very happy to show the images to her paramour. I'm hoping he might be able to at least point us in the right direction. I should be hearing back any day now."

Doria ran around the side of the desk and squeezed Cassie tightly. "I adore you."

"Yes. I know. I am adorable." She smirked at Doria. "But I am also selfish. I miss the shop and Miles just as much as you do. Elenor even more than me. She's just devastated thinking she may never get the chance to see Miles again."

"I," Doria was about to make a promise to Cassie that she would never let that happen. But these women had befriended her when she'd been nothing but bitter and unpleasant to Miles. She wanted to be as truthful with them as she could. "I hope it doesn't come to that."

"I understand. And so does Elenor. You aren't the one who did this to him. To us." Cassie wiped at the moisture collecting in her eyes. "Now, I've got work to do, and it looks like you've got some reading to do." Her eyes flicked to the tote slung over Doria's shoulder.

"We're going to take the long way home," Felicity said. "Maybe the stars will align and I'll finally get the chance to see this great bookstore you all are always on about." She winked at Cassie. "Then I'll make sure Doria relaxes tonight with a comfy blankie and a little light reading material.

2

JUST because Doria expected the shop to remain hidden as they walked home, didn't make her any less disappointed. While Cassie and Elenor insisted it was just the magic being tricky or spiteful, there was a teeny tiny voice whispering from the back of her mind saying what if it was Miles who was choosing this? What if he was unimpressed with their last interaction? What if his moral code was cemented firmly in mid last century and she seemed like a loose woman to him? What if, he wasn't all that different from other men and now that he'd gotten what he wanted from her, he was going to avoid her in the best way possible? Keeping the magical door closed to her forever.

What if Vespertine Books was at this very minute opening its door for some other young woman in the mood for a good book and a little bit more?

The what ifs would continue to mount despite her better intentions unless she put an end to them for good. She was, after all, a bit of a cynic. And the best way to quiet that part of her brain was to prove it was wrong. She would strive for positivity until she knew for certain.

At Fel's prompting, she grabbed a glass of merlot and ran a warm bath.

She sank into the water and reveled in the heat—almost too warm to be comfortable. She sipped her wine and brushed bubbles from the bottom of the glass before setting it on the ground outside the tub. The book of short fiction she'd nabbed earlier—by the author the mom buddies had suggested—was resting on the closed toilet seat. She wiped her hands on a towel and prayed to the gods of battered books not to drop the thing in the sudsy water. Then leaning back, she opened it to the first story in the volume. As the tension melted from her body with the heat, the wine, and the words, she dove in.

Merigold and the Three Brothers

Once upon a time in a realm where the known world bled into a land of magic and wonder, fae and human lives intertwined. It was in this place that light was shaped with shadows and fortune favored those who welcomed the mists of the fantastic. Nixies traveled the rivers and trolls mined the earth. Men were careful what they wished for, mindful that any word might be twisted and garbled by the magical beings close enough to hear and bored enough to play.

In the wilds of the forest, just to one side of an emerald swept glen, a spirited sprite named Merigold sought adventures in many forms. She danced with ogres and climbed trees filled with cats. She flirted with sorcerers and cried when leaves fell. She hunted for humans and seduced them with her voice and her beauty before spinning them about and sending them back to the far side of the glen to live out their days in constant want of her.

Oh. Doria's breath caught. Her mind immediately went to an image of Miles sitting forward, elbows on his knees, fully engaged in conversation with her. *I can't imagine being stuck with one choice for all eternity.* She'd argued that it was a lifetime, not eternity and he'd shrugged it off. If only she'd known then what he was battling.

When she'd pressed him further to describe what his favorite genre was he'd answered truthfully. *If I had to choose, I'd say true fantasy.*

15

Fairies and dark forests. Ogres, orcs, and magic that seeps into your bones and doesn't let go until you're stuck with the most delicious sort of book hangover.

This was that genre. Whether it contained the requisite sultry bits, spicy scenes, and good storytelling remained to be seen.

In addition to adventure, Merigold was fond of mirrors. In the shiny surfaces, she became enamored with her own mischief filled sapphire eyes and cascading gold and silver hair. Through them she not only witnessed her own striking features but also the magic of sprites long gone. There wasn't a mirror she could pass without wasting half a day lost in its enchantments.

One fateful day, while Merigold was gracefully dancing amidst the bluebells and belladonna, a gentle wind began to ruffle the ends of her hair. It sent the translucent strips of her gown twirling and tugged on her heart to listen to its words. She'd ventured further into the glen than on previous days and the wind whispered to her a warning. Just on the other side of the grassy hills and flowering trails, a small cottage sat. The cottage, the wind told her, was to be avoided at all costs. Humans lived there, the air said. Human brothers, who were not to be trifled with.

The breeze picked up and spoke to Merigold of misery and torment. The brothers had no fae lineage and were human through and through. They did not welcome the fantastic and would do all in their power to end any fun before it began.

Merigold was never one to shirk from a challenge and rather than heeding the wind's warning, she became convinced a visit to the cottage was sure to be filled with adventure and entertainment. If she was lucky, they might even have a mirror she could steal. No human before had resisted her seduction and these brothers were sure to be no different.

And so, Merigold pinched her cheeks and chewed on mint leaves as she bounced and swirled along with the bright spring air as it traversed the glen. Looking down, she adjusted the material of her gown. It was the softest pale lilac and the translucent material showed off her curves nicely. Had she planned the outing, she might have dusted her breast with gold to match the veining in her wings, but even without the added details, she knew the sight would be enough to capture even the strongest willed man or woman's attention.

Merigold had only ventured to the far side of the glen and the doorway to the human lands twice before. Once as a child, her father had taken her along as he sought to sour the milk in the cow of a man who had wronged him and once as a young woman. It was on the second trip that she had first come to appreciate the beauty held in a mirror. She'd never thought herself vane before, and still balked at the idea, but it was clear to her that even among the fairest of the fae, she was something special.

Stepping over the boundary of the glen, Merigold could just make out the rough outline of the cottage set back along the edge of the woods. Faint traces of wood smoke hung in the air and the sound of the morning birds was a symphony in her ears. Tucking her wings behind her, Merigold walked on bare feet over the lush carpet of pine needles and mossy stones.

As she approached the cottage, she took in the sight. It was a nicely kept place, even if it was a bit on the plain side. The shutters were tight and the doorstep was clean. A strong stone chimney rose from one side and the sprite could see a well-kept fence surrounding a meticulous garden in the back.

The mischievous know little fear, and Merigold was no different. Without a shred of shame, she walked up the pathway and to the front door. When she knocked and no one answered, it made all the sense in the world to simply push the door open and let herself in.

The interior of the cottage was much the same as the exterior. It was clean and tidy but furnished sparsely and with more thought to function than to beauty. A small sitting area held a worn oak bench along with a modest sofa and a bookshelf filled with leather-bound tomes. A sturdy table sat near the kitchen and around it sat four reasonable chairs. The hearth was still warm and the aroma of freshly baked bread filled the space.

A well-built staircase led to a loft of sorts. As Merigold placed her hand on the banister she wondered where the brothers might be. Perhaps she would make it to the top to find them all asleep in their beds. That might be fun. She quickened her pace up the steps only to be disappointed when she reached the top and found three cots, all neatly made, and not a brother in sight.

Her disappointment didn't last long, however. For standing in the corner Merigold spied a beautiful mirror framed in oak. It was nearly as tall as she was and gave her a splendid view of her creamy skin and long legs, as well as the shadows of sprite magic long since gone from the waking world. Shadows of wings flitted in and out of the frame, inviting her eyes to follow the dazzling trails left in their wake. As always, Merigold became mesmerized by the view in the glass and was lost to its secrets for hours.

It was only when she heard the front door open and the sounds of three hearty voices filling the cottage that she pulled her eyes from the mirror. The brothers were home and the fun was just about to begin.

Merigold floated toward the balcony and was intrigued by the sight of the brothers below. Despite wanting to rush down the stairs and work her magic on the men, she lingered taking in the sight. The door opened wider as the brothers entered, their rugged features illuminated by the warm glow of the lantern that one of them carried. Merigold held her breath as she watched them from atop her perch on the loft.

The naughty little sprite leaned forward, angling for a better view. Her breasts nearly spilled out of her top and her hair a wild conflagration of gold and silver, platinum and brushed bronze, highlights gleaming in the fading light. All the brothers needed to do was glance upward and they would be in for quite the eyeful.

The seconds stretched out deliciously. Would they be intimidated and fearful knowing she came from the far side of the glen? Would they see her in all her sprite beauty and simply lose control? Could she seduce them all at once and get them to do her bidding? In the past, she'd only stumbled upon single travelers, and alone one was easy enough to compel. But three? She was eager to see if she was up to the challenge.

Rather than walking down the stairs, Merigold decided to spread her lacy wings and hover at the top. Whether it was the noise or the motion that drew the first man's attention she couldn't be sure. But within seconds the tallest of the men let out a barely audible gasp. It was enough to get his brothers' attention and soon all three had eyes locked on her floating form.

The brothers stood at the foot of the stairs, three pairs of eyes widening, three sets of lips parting, and three sets of shoulders straightening. The brothers continued to stare at her, and gradually their faces transformed into three very different expressions. The first looked angry. The second, smitten.

The third, happily confused. But for all of their differences, she could tell she had surprised them, and the thought of it made her mouth water.

The view from atop the stairs was like a postcard of heaven. Vespertine clouds—

The book slipped from Doria's hands and only by sheer luck did she save it before it tumbled to its doom. Still, the bottom corner hit the surface and she winced knowing it would be warped and crinkled by the time the pages dried.

But Vespertine. Right there on the page. It had to be a simple coincidence, but given it was the first book she'd picked up to read solely for pleasure in the weeks since she last stepped foot in the shop, and it contained the cherished word? It sent her heart beating wildly. It wasn't a common word and yet here it was. When she needed the connection so desperately.

She decided it was a sign and continued to read.

The view from atop the stairs was like a postcard of heaven. Vespertine clouds, limned with rose and gold, were arcing up from the west like flaming ribbons and casting beautiful rays over the men standing below. Though she did not yet know their names, Merigold could feel the energy between them.

The air was laced with the aroma of pine and hemlock, a hint of sweet honey wine, and something else…something unknown but undeniably familiar.

One of the brothers stepped forward and swept his arm grandly toward a nearby table. It was the second of the brothers– the one who she seemed to have already transfixed with her presence. He was quite handsome for a mortal man, with broad shoulders and sandy brown hair. It was a shame really, for she knew already he would be too soft a challenge. Too easy to make the game much fun.

"Well," he said with a mischievous grin, a slight dimple forming along the right side of his mouth, "looks like we've got ourselves an unexpected guest."

Merigold smiled sweetly at him and blinked her eyelashes coquettishly. Setting her feet firmly upon the top step, she ran her hand along the smooth oak of the banister.

Looking up from under her lashes, she took one step down then paused, feigning a fear she certainly did not feel.

"I'm terribly sorry." Merigold filled her melodious voice with a slight tremor. "I don't mean to intrude. I fear I may be lost and was looking for shelter."

"And what manner of faerie folk are you then?" The first brother demanded. He appeared to be the oldest of the three, and while his face was still firmly lined with anger and mistrust, it did little to take away from his attractive features.

"Sprite," Merigold answered. "I am a woodland sprite."

"But sprites are meant to be tiny little things," the third brother replied. "And you're a full-grown woman."

Merigold flipped her hair over one shoulder and descended another step. If she happened to push her chest forward just as bit as she did so, who was to say? "Thank you for noticing. I can be tiny if I choose. But at the moment, I feel this might be a better fit." The third brother sucked in a sharp breath at the words.

"Indeed, it is." The second brother agreed, all but salivating on his boots. "Why don't you come all the way down and we can get better acquainted."

The eldest brother scoffed and Merigold stopped where she was on the steps, once again, filling her posture with timidity she didn't feel. It was all she could do to keep the smile from her face and the mischievous gleam from her eye.

"Pay no mind to Daniel," the third brother said. "He can get a bit bearish when he's hungry." Clearly the youngest of the men, he was still the most impressive. Standing a good head taller than his siblings, his face was dusted with stubble, and his forearms were roped with corded muscle. His hair curled boyishly around the base of his neck and caught the sunlight. While his look of confusion had

cleared somewhat, his easy smile held the barest trace of caution.

Merigold took another step down. "You are Daniel?" She asked the eldest brother. He crossed his arms over his chest and nodded, the scowl never leaving his face.

Doria could certainly relate to Daniel. She'd be none too happy if some rando showed up in her place. Even if he were the most gorgeous man she'd ever seen. Normal people didn't just break and enter and then wait for you to fall madly in love with them.

"And you?" She smiled sweetly at the second brother.

"Dominic," he answered quickly.

She looked to the third and youngest of the men.

"My name is Derek. Now that we have shared our names, perhaps you might tell us yours."

Merigold blinked at the third and youngest of the men. "My name is Merigold."

She descended the last few steps and placed her hands behind her back, rocking up onto her tiptoes. She noted with some satisfaction how both Daniel and Dominic's eyes drifted over her with the movement. And while Daniel didn't share his brother's open hunger, he took his time in taking in her ivory skin and full curves.

Though his eyes never left her face, the youngest brother, Derek, stepped forward and reached out his hand for hers. With a gentle smile, he said, "It's nice to meet you, Merigold. We weren't expecting any visitors today."

Merigold allowed Derek to take her hand in his own. She couldn't help but drink him in; his tousled hair catching the light of the sun and his bright smile making him look even more inviting than before.

The eldest brother cleared his throat and stepped between them. "Now that we have shared our names," he said gruffly, "perhaps you might tell us what brings you here."

Before Merigold could answer, Derek cut in with an affable grin directed at both Merigold and Daniel alike.

"Ah come on now Daniel," Derek teased good-naturedly. "Surely we can offer this lovely lady some hospitality while we hear what it is she seeks."

"I'd like to stay here." Merigold walked away from Derek and traced her hand along the table, drawing little circles in the moisture there. "At least for the night."

"Of course, you can stay," Dominic blurted. "For the night. For the week. For forever if you like." He glanced sideways at Daniel with a knowing smirk before turning back to the sprite.

"I don't think forever will be necessary," Daniel grumbled. "I'll put the soup on. Dominic, fetch the wine. Derek, perhaps you can warm up the bath water so we can all clean ourselves up before we eat."

"And what shall I do?" Merigold asked.

Merigold looked around the room, unsure of how to make herself seem useful. She was used to taking care of herself, but here in this strange house, she was in unfamiliar territory. In the woods things were different. While she'd come here with a purpose, she was still more off kilter than she would have liked.

"Well," Derek said with a smirk, "I suppose we can always use an extra hand." He gestured to the cookware on the counter. "Would you mind helping Daniel prepare dinner?"

Merigold nodded eagerly. "Of course, I would be happy to help!"

The kitchen was a room both beautiful and functional. The stone walls held in the warmth and had been kept free of grime and dust. A large cupboard covered with intricate carvings took up a good portion of one wall. A small woodstove sat next to it. Adjacent to the kitchen, on the other side of the long table and oak bench, sat the hearth. It appeared newer than the rest of the structure, but what did Merigold know of human cottages? The entire space was cast in a warm glow from the dancing flames of the hearth and a series of candles, which rested on top of the table.

Merigold looked to the hearth where Derek was stoking the fire. He'd carried a large wooden tub over and was dumping steaming water from a metal pot into the half-full tub. Merigold felt a flush creep up her neck as she watched the strong muscles in his arms and shoulders as he worked. As if sensing her stare, he looked up and a lazy grin spread across his face. He winked at her then straightened and walked to the entrance with the pot in hand. Merigold returned her gaze to the carrots in front of her and soon heard the creaking of metal that she assumed was a water pump of some sort. A few minutes later the door banged shut again and Derek placed the pot above the flames.

When the temperature seemed to his liking, he stripped off his shirt and began washing with a small cloth. Merigold was fascinated– both by this primitive means of bathing and his beautifully sculpted body. Whenever Merigold needed a bath, she simply swam naked through a stream or hot spring. This was completely new to her.

Once again Derek caught her watching him. His grin grew even broader as he took his time scrubbing every inch of exposed skin. Merigold was growing warmer by the minute. Her wings began to flutter in time with her rapid pulse. She was supposed to be doing the seducing, not the other way around. Straightening her spine and calming her wings, she turned away from Derek but felt his warm chuckle even as her back was turned.

She needed to focus and cooking was a good way to do it. With the smell of sweet onions and roasting meat, Merigold's stomach began to rumble. It took more than beautiful mirrors and plans for trickery to sustain her, and she hadn't eaten anything since arriving at the cottage. She quickly diced the remaining vegetables, her fingers deftly using the knife Daniel had handed her.

The sound of a cork being popped and the heady smell of strong wine drew her attention just as a warm hand ran from her shoulder to her elbow, lingering there for a moment. "Here you are my lovely thing." Dominic stood with his arm outstretched and a wooden goblet of wine extended to her.

Derek had disappeared again. Daniel gave the soup a good stir and then turned to study his brother. The look on his face had Dominic scrambling to hand over his goblet of wine and then fetch another for himself. Merigold took a tentative sip from her cup. The wine was strong and sweet. Dominic raised his goblet in salute and grinned, the corners of his eyes crinkling. Merigold watched as he took a long drink from his cup and wiped the back of his hand across his mouth. His eyes hadn't left her and his expression told her exactly what he was thinking.

Daniel hadn't spoken much during the meal preparation, but he hadn't seemed quite as hostile toward her either. Now looking at his brother, his expression hardened once again. "Dominic, why don't you get cleaned up? You smell like the back end of a mule."

Dominic flinched then turned a bright crimson. He threw a filthy look at his brother but hurried over to where Derek had left the washbasin. Glowering, he pulled his shirt over his head. He turned to glance at Merigold, his glower morphing into something between longing and preening. She smiled politely then turned back toward Daniel. If Dominic thought she'd be in awe of his bare chest, he was mistaken. Merigold had grown up on the far side of the glen. The people there were beautiful beyond compare. The men glorious and strong. While Dominic was handsome enough, he was no fae warrior. And he was nothing compared to his youngest brother.

Daniel nodded to the wooden bench next to him. "Have a seat."

Merigold dropped onto the bench and was immediately struck by how uncomfortable it was. The wood had no give at all. She wiggled to try and make herself more comfortable, but it only served to put more pressure on her legs and backside.

"No hard wood where you come from?" Daniel raised an eyebrow at the sprite. The words sounded teasing, but his features still held no joy.

"Plenty actually." She quipped back.

"Well. You can wiggle all you like. It isn't going to get any softer."

"Are we still talking about the bench?" Merigold teased.

"I don't know. You tell me."

Merigold hid her smirk behind her cup. Perhaps the wind had been wrong. This didn't seem much of a challenge at all.

A loud splash drew both their attention. "Almost done there?" Derek asked and was rewarded by a string of obscenities from Dominic.

Daniel blew out a long breath. "I supposed I should get cleaned up too. Keep an eye on the soup, would you?"

Merigold nodded and rose from the bench. Stirring the pot, she inhaled the rich aroma. Her stomach gave a long rumble and she remembered again how she'd spent her day upstairs. Thoughts of the looking glass had her smiling brightly. Perhaps if all went to plan, she'd be able to convince the men to let her keep it. Maybe they'd even haul it to the edge of the glen for her.

"That's the first real smile I've seen since you made your appearance." Suddenly Derek was right next to her, his own cup of wine at his lips.

"How do you mean?" Her smile turned to a frown.

"We've seen the shy smile, the seductive smile, the I'm trying to look sweet and timid smile, but that is the first real smile you've had since we came home to find you here. Tell me little sprite, what makes you smile like that?"

Merigold thought about denying all the things he'd said but decided against it. Derek was clearly the most observant of the three and she had no interest in lying over something so small.

"I was thinking of the lovely mirror you have upstairs."

"That's certainly not what I thought you were going to say."

Merigold chuckled. "It's a very nice mirror."

"It is. It was our mother's. A gift from our father on the day they were married." Merigold's face fell. If it were an heirloom, she'd be a fool to think they'd just give it away. "Tell me Merigold, what do you see when you look in the mirror?"

She answered immediately with little thought or hesitation. "I see a beautiful sprite."

"Is that all?"

"It's enough." She turned from him but he grabbed at her wrist and leaned into her.

His breath was warm against her ear as he whispered against it. "I hope the next time you gaze into the glass, it'll be more than enough."

The bath water had gone cold.

Doria hadn't bothered to grab a bookmark, so she rested the paperback open face down, splayed to keep her place, on the countertop while she grabbed a towel. Hurrying to dry off and get into her comfiest pajamas, she thought back to the strange turn of events her life had taken recently.

If she'd picked up this book just a handful of weeks ago, she wouldn't have made it past the second page before either donating it back to the library or giving it away. But after Miles insisted she broaden her reading horizons, she was starting to embrace the idea that one could read several different genres and if not love them, at least enjoy them a bit.

She didn't love this story so far, but she was the tiniest bit proud that she was at least giving it a chance.

She grabbed the book and her wine and got comfortable on the couch. With any luck, the ending would be fantastic and she'd go to sleep satisfied with the story.

Merigold made her way up the stairs, grateful for a place to rest her head. The brothers had offered her one of the cots in their room and she chose the bed closest to the beautiful mirror, feeling strangely drawn to it. She glanced at it but didn't stare for long. The image was as it always was. A beautiful sprite and shadowed wings. Nothing new. Nothing different.

She collapsed into the cot and relished in its comfort. After a moment, she realized Derek was behind her. She turned from the glass and looked up at him. He didn't say anything, just crossed his arms over his broad chest.

She raised an eyebrow in question.

"Looks like I'll be sleeping on the floor," Derek said with a shrug.

Merigold felt almost guilty. "Is this one yours?" She gestured to the cot with her chin.

"It is," Derek said quietly as he reached out and grasped a lock of her hair between his fingers before letting it go again with a sigh. "But not tonight. Tonight, it's yours." He let the strand of hair fall from his grasp and grabbing a blanket from the trunk at the foot of the bed, he turned and left her.

Merigold heard Derek's footsteps as he made his way down the stairs. She was still staring at the flames of the candles, her thoughts clear and uncluttered in their quiet reverie when Daniel and Dominic came up.

Daniel dropped into his bed after a glance her way and Dominic stared at her for a long moment, open hunger in his eyes.

"I'm blowing out the candle Dom, if you know what's good for you, you'll be in your bed by the time I do," Daniel announced gruffly.

Dominic glanced away from Merigold and took a few steps toward his own cot before turning back to look at her one more time. "Goodnight Merigold," he whispered before disappearing under his blankets.

True to his word, Daniel snuffed out the remaining candles, and the space was plunged into near total darkness. Merigold felt her cheeks heat up as she lay down on the cot and drew the covers up over herself, feeling oddly exposed suddenly with three men in such proximity. Her plan was working so far, but what would she do when she had them all enamored? Perhaps the wind was right. Perhaps she'd been a fool to come here. She lay awake for a long time before finally drifting off to sleep.

Merigold awoke the next morning to an empty room. The brothers were gone, leaving the cottage in a state of eerie peace. Frowning, Merigold shifted and saw a small bouquet of wildflowers resting on her pillow. Fondly, she recalled Derek's words from the night before and smiled down at the flowers. This small gesture made her heart swell with warmth even though her chest felt hollow knowing they had left without saying goodbye.

The game had lost its fun. She'd already captured Dominic's affection and Daniel—despite his hard demeanor was crumbling too. But it was Derek she felt guilt over. She didn't want to hurt him she realized. There was only one way to fix the mess she created.

Resigned to their departure, she took one last longing look at the mirror before abandoning the cottage for her home across the glen.

As she walked down the path, a light rain began to fall, giving way to unrelenting thunder and lightning that lit up the sky like fireworks.

The rain had been falling steadily for the past few hours, sending streams of water over the trees and glen. Merigold stood still in the middle of it all, embracing the deluge that soaked her to the bone. With a whoop and a yell, she spun around and laughed, enjoying the freedom of the moment. She felt something shift inside her as she let go of her worries and fears and simply danced.

The gossamer fabric of her gown clung tightly to her curves, her hair was drenched, and water was running in rivulets down her body. Turning her face up to the downpour she relished in the feeling of being alive as she twirled about in dizzying circles.

Suddenly there were strong arms around her, pulling her close and enveloping her in warmth- Derek's warmth. He'd been careful to reach under her wings so as not to crush the sensitive gossamer. Had he followed her from the cottage without her knowing it, watching from afar as she let down all inhibitions and allowed herself to feel joy again?

Derek quickly spun Merigold to face him, her body pressed against his and she could feel the heat radiating from his chest. Merigold gasped as her body rubbed against his chest, the thin fabric doing little to keep her skin from his.

Without thinking, Merigold rose on her toes and captured his mouth with her own.

A moan escaped him. The sound nearly drove her wild. He broke the kiss and stared down at her upturned face. Then, without warning, he crushed her lips in a hungry kiss that sent sparks through her veins and an urge to move closer to him. With one hand gripping the fabric of her dress at the small of her back and the other exploring her body, he nipped at her lower lip. Merigold felt like she was melting into him.

The rain continued to pour down around them as Derek pulled the fabric of her dress lower until it pooled at her feet. His hands roamed hungrily over every inch of exposed skin, sending shivers throughout her entire body. Then it was her turn. She tore at his clothing, the buttons and buckles coming loose with her frantic movements. When he at last stepped out of his clothing, she marveled at the sight of him standing naked in the warm rain. The evidence of his need for her was on full display.

Stepping close to him again, he took her in his arms, trailing kisses from her ear, down her neck, before reaching her breast. Merigold swayed with the feel of it and Derek caught her easily, twisting with her in the glorious storm. Together they moved in harmony as if they'd been dancing this way their entire lives. Their movements grew more intense as they reveled in each other's touch, pleasure rising with each caress until Merigold thought she'd burst from ecstasy.

The rain cascaded off them both as they explored each other's bodies, making love under the open sky. Merigold felt euphoric, and she imagined that the drops falling from the sky were filled with magic. It was as if Derek infused every cell in her body with life and light until she thought she'd explode with pleasure.

The sun began to peek through the clouds and Derek held her close for a moment longer before finally pulling away with a satisfied smile on his face. He rose and retrieved his clothes, dressing in the sodden material. Merigold didn't bother. She was out in nature and being free of the damp fabric was what she needed.

"You'll need to put something on, or I'm afraid we won't make it very far before I'm going to need you again." Derek's smile was wide and open.

Merigold didn't answer the teasing.

"Come," he urged gently, beckoning her towards the cottage. When Merigold stayed rooted to the spot, his brow furrowed in confusion.

"I can't follow you just yet," she declared firmly. "Not until I know what I should do next."

The expression on his face was pained. "What do you mean?"

Merigold hesitated for a moment, looking deeply into Derek's eyes. She saw the love and understanding there and knew that whatever she asked he would give her. With newfound strength, she nodded her head.

"I need some time," Merigold started slowly, "to decide what to do with Dominic and Daniel. They both want something from me, but their approaches are so different...Daniel is so hard and Dominic is too hungry for something I don't want to give."

Oh my god. Doria stopped reading and flipped the book to read the back jacket. Was this one of those reverse harem books where one woman fell for several men and they all lived happily sex filled days together? It didn't say that in the blurb, but the blurb wasn't very descriptive.

She wanted to be open-minded, but she wasn't sure she was ready for the deep end of the pool just yet.

It's fine, she told herself. *If it is, I can get through it.*

"Well, I hadn't planned on sharing you with either of them."

"Do they know that? I feel like they have other ideas."

"I can deal with my brothers." He drew a finger down the lacey edge of her wing and she shuddered at his touch.

The sky overhead was clearing and birdsong could be heard filling the glen. A warm breeze blew through her hair, and she felt it caress the bare skin of her legs.

Derek reached out and cupped her face in his hands. "Take as much time as you need," he said softly, "Just promise me you'll come back."

Merigold smiled coyly and leaned closer until their lips touched in a soft kiss. When they finally broke apart, she whispered," I promise."

Right. Maybe not a reverse harem then. Crisis averted.
She continued to read.

Merigold had been away from the cottage for a few days, but she couldn't stop thinking about Derek and her feelings for him. She'd always been the one to do the seducing, but he seemed to have turned the tables on her.

And then there were his brothers - Dominic and Daniel. They were so different than Derek. Dominic was too eager to please while Daniel was too stern and demanding. But they both wanted something from her that she wasn't sure she wanted to give.

The forest had always been her refuge. The leaves crunched as she strode, and the earth soaked up the water misted from her feet. A few feet away sounds muted; a few yards more the trees arching above hid the sky from view, and the rest of the world faded into insignificance. She wanted for nothing when she floated among the trees, but now she seemed at a loss. The flowers didn't smell as sweet, the air didn't taste as rich, and the wind didn't sound as enchanting.

Merigold thought back to when she first saw the cottage and the beautiful mirror inside it. Something about it pulled at her like a magnet, and although she was still uncertain why, Merigold felt a strange sense that if she could gaze into its dark depths one last time, perhaps the answers she was seeking would become clear.

After agonizing over her inability to get Derek and his brothers as well as the mirror and its hidden secrets out of her mind, she crossed the glen.

As she trudged up the familiar path to the cottage, Merigold's heart raced with anticipation. Throwing open the door, she barreled up the stairs, her breath coming in short gasps. She came to stand before the mirror and gazed deep into the darkness of its glass. Her face - still as lovely as ever - was no longer recognizable. Gone was the vain sprite. Gone was the untouchable seductress. Gone was the stubborn and lonely woman who played with others without a care. It was as if she had never existed at all. Her selfishness and frivolity had been replaced by acceptance and love. Merigold understood that love was its own kind of temptress and she was more than willing to let it claim her if it meant she could spend her days with the youngest of the brothers—the perfect man who had captured her heart.

Is that what the wind had meant all those days ago? That coming here would ruin the selfish creature she'd once been? If so, she was happy to have not heeded its warning.

Just as she'd felt it days prior in the glen, Merigold felt a warmth behind her. Hands clasped around her shoulders and she knew without turning around it was Derek. He radiated a strength and protection that she had never known before, and for the first time in what seemed like years, she felt safe.

She nestled deeper into his embrace and Derek kissed the back of her head gently, as if he were trying to memorize the shape of her. He smelled like smoke and salt, earthy and sweet. Merigold felt all her worries drift away. She looked up at him through the mirror's reflection, his face full of admiration for her beauty. The tenderness in his eyes made her heart flutter and without thinking, she leaned into him, twisting her head back and up to kiss him softly on the lips. It felt like the world stopped moving as their lips locked together and Merigold could have sworn the mirror changed. The dark glass lighter than it had been.

The kiss lingered until Derek finally pulled away, looking deep into Merigold's eyes with an intensity that made heat rise to her cheeks. He didn't say anything - words weren't needed - but simply held onto her tightly as if he never wanted to let go again. At that moment, Merigold knew what true emotion felt like - and how easily it could consume you if you let it get too close.

Merigold turned around to face Derek, the glass of the mirror reflecting their deep love for one another and the strength in his arms holding her close.

"I've talked to my brothers," Derek said. "Daniel is happy to have extra help around the cottage."

Merigold smiled, relieved that at least one of them had been welcoming.

"What of Dominic?" she asked tentatively.

Derek sighed. "He was unhappy, but he says he'll come to accept it in time. If not, he says he'll move on."

Merigold nodded slowly, understanding that even if Dominic didn't fully accept that she would never be his, he was willing to try to be happy for them. She looked back up into Derek's eyes and smiled softly at what she saw there - love and acceptance - then returned his embrace tighter than before, grateful for him and all that he was willing to do for her.

"When you look in the mirror now, do you like what you see?" Derek asked softly as if reading her mind.

"Very much," she replied without hesitation.

"And is it enough?"

Yes." Merigold said as he kissed the top of her head. "It is more than enough."

Hmm.
Doria tilted her head and sighed.

As much as she wanted to like the story, she just *didn't*.

It wasn't the genre or the setting or the sex. It just didn't feel like one she could connect with. Did that make her a terrible person again? She wasn't sure.

What she really wanted after putting the book aside was to talk to Miles. Maybe he could shed some unseen light on the plot or the premise. Maybe she was missing the point.

Not sure what else to do with herself, and having no one to discuss the book with, Doria went to bed feeling distinctly dissatisfied.

3

THE sidewalk in front of Doria was slick with morning dew and moss. She had to be careful not to slip in the new pumps she was wearing. They were red and matched the polka dots on her dress. It wasn't her usual garb, but for some reason, she felt she should look nice.

The sun hadn't yet risen, but the sky held the peculiar shades of peach and green, lavender and grey that signaled the coming dawn. Up ahead of her, a large orange cat jumped from a trash bin and into her path. It turned its glowing eyes on her and gave a long slow blink. She smiled at it in return. The feline turned its head and Doria followed the animal's gaze.

Her heart thumped. There it was. Battered and worn but oh so beautiful. The wooden sign read Vespertine Books.

After weeks of searching, it had finally reappeared. She had the barest sense of the cat slinking away in her periphery as she pushed through the unlocked door.

The bell had been replaced by a gong and the noise it made at her entry was deafening. She cringed at the clatter even as she ran forward into the dimly lit space.

"Miles!" Her voice was little more than a croak. "Miles. Where are you?"

She rounded the front counter and hurried past her favorite chair. It would have been too much to ask for him to be sitting and reading quietly at the front of the shop. He must have been back in the stacks somewhere, shelving and arranging books.

She jogged past the front shelves and headed toward the back. "Miles. It's me. Where the hell are you?" She was breathless with anticipation. He had to be here somewhere.

Faint humming sounded from the next row over, but when she turned the corner, he wasn't there. She could still hear the tune—vaguely familiar and growing louder—always coming from the next row over.

"Miles stop playing around." Her voice cracked and Doria knew she was close to tears.

"Don't cry." His voice was right behind her. "It took me a minute to realize you were here."

Doria spun around and crashed into his chest. Immediately his arms were around her and the tears were well and truly falling.

"Shh. Doria." He cradled her to him. "I'm here."

He released his embrace and placed both of his hands on her face, tilting her chin up and wiping the tears away with the pads of his thumbs.

Doria took a shuddering breath and then pulled him down to kiss him. He returned the kiss with just as much longing. When they finally broke apart, Doria used the back of her hand to wipe the snot from her nose. Then she placed both hands on his chest and pushed him backward.

"Where the hell have you been?" she demanded. "I've tried and tried to find you, but the door hasn't been here."

Miles took off his glasses and rubbed at the bridge of his nose. Had he been wearing his glasses when she kissed him? She couldn't recall.

"How long has it been?" he asked.

Doria looked at him in confusion.

"How long has it been?" he repeated. "Since you saw me last?"

He didn't know? How was it he didn't know?

"Four weeks and three days," she answered frowning.

"Over a month." He blew out a long breath and tilted his head back to look up at the ceiling. "Over a month since we. . ."

"Had sex?" she prompted.

He grimaced and nodded. "I had no idea it had been that long."

"What do you mean?"

Miles took her hand and led her back past the counter and the small sitting area there. She looked around but her favorite chair was missing.

"I didn't know it had been that long since I had a visitor. No one's been here since that night," Miles explained. "I was beginning to wonder. Even if you didn't come back, I expected to see Cassondra at some point."

"She couldn't find the door either," Doria said. "Even Elenor's tried."

Dropping onto the sofa, Doria toed off her sneakers and pulled her jean-clad legs up under her.

That wasn't right. She'd been wearing a dress. With red dots. To match her red shoes.

"Miles? Where's my favorite chair?"

"You tell me. It's your dream Doria." He sat next to her. Hands on his knees and black tattoo peeking out from the cuff of his sleeve.

No. It couldn't be a dream. She'd waited so long to see him. She wanted the real Miles. Not a dream version her mind had contrived to make her feel better.

"Just because it's a dream, doesn't mean it isn't the real me," he said calmly. "Don't you remember?"

She did remember. She'd dreamt of him before and he'd shared the same experience. In the waking world, they'd both recalled the conversation clearly. Was this the same?

"Are you sure?" she asked. "I've been thinking about you a lot. And I read a book last night. One you probably love. It might just be my subconscious playing with me."

"I'm as sure as I can be. What book?"

She told him the title and he barked out a laugh. "You read that? Willingly?"

She snuggled up next to him. "I did. And I want you to tell me why I should love it as much as everyone else does."

"I'm not sure you should. It wasn't particularly good in my opinion." He said the words into her hair.

She sat up and turned to look into his eyes. "Really? But it was a full-blown fantasy. Sprites and a magical forest and everything? Plus, a little steamy. I thought for sure. . ."

He raised an eyebrow. "Do you love every grisly horror and fast-paced thriller ever written?"

"Well no. Obviously not. But the women at the book sale said it was all over social media. Everyone loves her books they said." She chewed at her lower lip.

"Not every book by every author is for everyone. I don't like her stuff at all. Not my taste."

Hearing him admit this made her feel warm and fuzzy. Maybe she wasn't a terrible person after all. This was exactly why she needed someone like Miles to discuss her reading adventures with. But Miles wasn't actually there and it was just a dream.

All of a sudden, the warm and fuzzy feeling evaporated and in its wake, a deep loneliness dug in.

"I want to see you again," she said as she sank deeper into his shoulder.

"You're seeing me now. Try to enjoy the moment."

"It isn't the same."

"Look at me, Doria." He placed his hand under her chin and tilted her face up. "I can't promise you things will work out. I've been in this limbo for so long, that I'd forgotten to hope. Then you showed up and things got a little bit brighter. I'm not willing to give up on us just yet."

He dipped his mouth down and brushed his lips whisper soft against hers. The act was softer than butterfly wings against her skin, but it sent a shiver through her entire body. Arching up, she placed a hand on the back of his neck and pulled him closer before kissing him back. Dragging her mouth down his jaw, she teased his skin with tongue and teeth. Miles' breath came quicker and he moaned as she drew his earlobe into her mouth.

In a fluid motion, he pulled back and grabbed her hips, dragging her body down on the sofa beneath him. Then he was repaying her kisses with his own brand of sweet torment, trailing his tongue over her collarbone to the small notch at the base of her throat. His hands worked their way up under her shirt to the underside of her breasts, where he allowed his fingertips to trace the outline of her bra.

Doria shifted beneath him, wanting him closer. Needing to feel his skin against hers. She wrapped her legs around his waist and sighed as he pushed against her with his thigh. Frantic now, she grabbed at the front of his shirt, fingers fumbling as they tried to undo the buttons.

Miles laughed as she cursed with the effort.

"Not funny," she breathed.

Miles shifted above her and his face faded as cracks of light shone through him. He frowned as a beam of sunshine speared through him and onto Doria's chest.

"No" she cried. "No, not yet Miles."

"It's," he shook his head. "I'll see you soon." He tried to smile, but it was a broken desperate thing.

Tears leaked from Doria's eyes as Miles dissolved into beams of muted light.

She scrubbed the heels of her hands into her eyes and when she pulled them away, the cozy seating area, the front desk, and shelves of books were gone. Doria was alone in her bed, the morning sun streaming through the blinds.

A week went by and then two.

The entrance to Vespertine Books remained elusive.

Doria worked most days and wandered the streets of town most evenings. She kept in touch with Cassondra every couple of days, hoping Miles' niece would get a lead on the tattoo and its possible language or meaning.

Twice more she dreamt of Miles, but on both occasions, the encounter was fleeting. A bare glimpse of him as he sailed away on a ship in the distance and a terrible nightmare where he was trapped in an iron casket being lowered into the earth. On both occasions, she woke with a racing heart and a horrible feeling of helplessness that only faded as the dreams flitted away with the morning light.

She was finishing up at the café one afternoon when her phone pinged with a message from Cassie. It seemed as though her contact at the university had come through. Doria agreed to head to Elenor's home that evening.

She sent Felicity a message inviting her along, then swung by her favorite market for a tub of spinach and artichoke dip, a sliced baguet, grapes, and a bottle of sparkling wine. She figured they'd either need to celebrate or drown their sorrows after Cassie shared whatever news she'd gotten. Doria was hoping for a celebration.

She met up with Felicity outside their building and the pair walked the short distance to Elenor's. The insects were loud and the tourists louder.

Elenor and Cassie were waiting for them on the porch when they arrived. Elenor had a pitcher of gin spritzers ready and waiting. She patted Doria on the cheek as she handed her a glass. "Let's save the bubbly stuff for later." She winked and led them all inside.

Cassie grabbed some plates and set out a platter of fried pickles alongside rosemary glazed chicken thighs and a bowl of scrumptious looking beet salad. Felicity unloaded the food Doria had picked up and they all heaped up their plates.

"You all dig in," Cassie said as she retrieved a sheaf of papers and put her reading glasses on. "I want to make sure I've got this all right. It's a little convoluted, to be honest."

"I hope your friend didn't feel too put upon with the whole thing," Doria said.

Cassie dipped her chin and looked over her glasses at Doria. "Please. The woman lives for drama, I can assure you. And as it happens, her man was quite thrilled with the translation. He asked if he could keep a set of photos and possibly write it up for a presentation. I told him to hold off until we knew what we were dealing with. The last thing anybody needs is some mass curse going out on a bunch of unsuspecting academicians."

Elenor barked a laugh and Felicity giggled along with her.

Doria just sighed and shook her head.

"Oh, come on Peaches. If you don't laugh, you'll cry," her roommate stated before stuffing her mouth with a heaping forkful of beets and goat cheese.

"Now, Cassie. What do we need to do to free that uncle of mine?" The words sounded so odd coming from the older woman. As far as Doria was concerned, Miles was a handsome young man in the prime of his life. He didn't look more than twenty-seven or twenty-eight years old and even though Doria knew he was decades older, it was so hard to grasp.

Cassie snapped the pages and got right to it. "Well according to Geoffrey, the tattoo was a relatively easy puzzle for him to solve. He says the reason it looks so foreign, is because it isn't all one language at all. It's a mix of three. Two dead ones—Docian and Akkadian—mixed in with standard old English. There's a pattern to it, I guess. He says something about a repeating numerical pattern and the way the words tie together. Most people wouldn't recognize the dead languages at all, particularly the Docian because only a few examples of it have been found and those were mainly plant names or something."

Doria had heard of Akkadian before in one of her library courses. She thought it was close to Sumerian but couldn't be certain. Even old English was quite unusual. It didn't sound like the modern tongue at all. No wonder she hadn't recognized it.

"Yes, that's all very interesting," Elenor tutted, "but what does it *say?*"

"I'm getting there," Cassie said. She sipped her spritzer and continued. "It reads like a set of verse apparently. A riddle maybe. Or…"

"A spell." Doria supplied.

"Yes." Cassie agreed. "If we're thinking Peter did this intentionally, I'm sure you're right."

Doria sat forward. "Miles told me he was into arcane things. Books and dark stuff."

"Right. This translation is the best he could come up with." She flipped to the second page of her notes and snapped the paper. "*In the endless day of the eternal season, life will give to life. So one may walk unending, the other shall remain. No fire or steal or penned prose shall end the bond, but if words of merit are born from hate, only then will time be restored.*"

"Well damn. What the hell does that mean?" Felicity asked.

Cassie shook her head. "I have no idea."

"Read it again, dear," Elenor said.

"In the endless day of the eternal season," Cassie read slowly.

"That could mean where Miles is stuck? He doesn't age, so maybe that's the endless day?" Doria mused.

"Life will give to life."

Doria shook her head. She had no idea what that was referring to.

"So one may walk unending, the other shall remain."

Again, not a clue. She looked to the others and they seemed just as perplexed.

"No fire or steal or penned prose shall end the bond."

"Whatever the bond is, it wouldn't be easy to break," Elenor said and Doria agreed. That part was pretty clear.

"But if words of merit are born from hate, only then will time be restored." Cassie took her reading glasses off and set them on top of her papers as she finished. "That's the bit that gets me. It's as if this last line is the key to freeing him or restoring him to time, but

I'm not sure what the words of merit would be. Is there another spell hidden in the shop somewhere do you think?"

"Maybe if we find it, he just needs to read the words aloud and the curse will be broken," Felicity said excitedly.

Doria groaned. "Maybe, but that seems too easy. Plus, even if it is hidden inside Vespertine Books, we can't get in to look. It's as if the curse knew something and is keeping him hidden all of a sudden."

Doria wanted to kick a wall, she was so frustrated. "I will tell you this. If I see that little knob Peter Smith, I'm not sure I'll be able to keep from doing something terrible."

"You and me both dear." Elenor drained the last of her gin spritzer and poured herself another.

The days continued to tick by and with each sunset, Doria was frustrated that she'd failed at both finding the hidden doorway and teasing out the meaning of the spell. In contrast, she was hopeful Miles would magically appear in her dreams. Unfortunately, he remained elusive in the real world and as well as in her head. The longer she went without seeing him the more she began to believe her dream of him hadn't been a real connection at all.

Sitting on the park bench with Felicity, she studied her phone and the picture she'd taken of Cassie's notes. The sun was high overhead and the shade of the oak tree they'd claimed earlier was shrinking by the minute. Soon it would be too hot to stay and she'd be left to trudge home alone while her roommate flitted off on another afternoon movie date.

"Let's talk through it one more time," Fel said as she leaned forward to peer at the small screen.

"Why do I feel as if it should be so obvious? God, I suck at puzzles and riddles," Doria bemoaned.

"You and me both Peaches."

They ran through a dozen possibilities, each more ludicrous than the last. But in the end, wasn't the entire thing ludicrous? Doria never in her wildest imagination, would have believed she'd become central to such an unbelievable plot. Some morning, she woke, completely convinced Miles hadn't existed at all and her memories of the bookshop were just precursors to her losing her mind. Then she'd remember the feel of his hands on her body and the soft caress of his lips and know there was no possible way she could conjure those from nothing.

Without making any more progress in sorting out the curse, she huffed a sigh and put her phone back in her purse.

"You should get going or you'll be all hot and sweaty for your date."

Felicity raised her arm and grimaced at the damp ring staining the gray material of her sundress. "Too late for that. The pit stains are for real."

Doria laughed and batted a hand at her friend. "I'm sure," she paused. "What's his name again?"

"Landon."

"Right. It's tough to keep up. I'm sure Landon won't mind at all."

Felicity shrugged as if to say, if he does that's on him.

Doria was just about to hug her goodbye when she caught sight of Peter Smith skulking around the edge of the park. Was the bastard following her? Doria didn't understand why he would continue to pop up otherwise.

She jumped up and tore after him without a thought, Felicity this time close on her heels. As soon as he saw them, he hurried out the gate and back up the street. Doria wasn't about to let him get away this time.

He rounded the corner by the bar and Doria realized he was heading toward the site where the bookshop had once stood waiting for her, tucked unobtrusively between the used appliance shop and the clothing store. Sprinting after him, her heart pounded with the idea he might just lead her to the doorway. Even if she didn't catch him, she might get something even better.

But as she took the last turn up the bustling street and past the small alcove, she had her hopes set on, her heart fell. Peter had once again escaped and the bookshop remained just as stubbornly absent as always.

Doria stifled the urge to scream. It felt as if Peter was toying with her—showing up for her to glimpse and then vanishing into thin air.

Breathless, Felicity jogged to a halt next to her. "Where. . . did. . .he go?"

"Fuck if I know." Doria turned to her friend. "I don't know how much more of this I can take, Fel."

Felicity wrapped her in an overly sweaty embrace. "You're the toughest cookie I know."

"Yeah, whatever."

Felicity stepped back and pulled on Doria's arm. "I need to get going soon, but as I was realizing how desperately out of shape I am while running, the blood flow must have done something to my brain."

Doria frowned. "Okay."

"I was just thinking, Peter Smith moves pretty fast for a man who is reportedly a few years older than Miles. That would put him close to the century mark, yeah?"

"Well yes, but what does that have to—" Doria stopped mid-sentence.

. . .life will give to life. So one may walk unending, the other shall remain.

"Oh, you brilliant, beautiful woman." Doria drew Felicity in and gave her a wet smacking kiss on the lips.

It was so obvious now. However the curse magic was working, by keeping Miles locked in eternal stagnation within the bookshop, Peter Smith was drawing his own eternal youth and life force from it. He Probably hadn't aged a day more than Miles, but he was at least free to wander the outside world. It was brilliant in its cruelty.

Felicity cringed as a giggle burst from her lips. "Don't get too excited. Even if it means what we think it means, you still don't know how the end works—how to break the curse completely."

"Not yet we don't, but it's only a matter of time until we do."

4

IT HAD been a long day already when Doria's replacement at the café called out sick. She'd been on her feet for hours but at the pleading of her manager Ricko, she agreed to stay and work the dinner rush too. It was an easy sell, considering how badly she needed the money. Maybe if she'd had plans for the night, or someone to go home to, she would have declined, but as it was, she couldn't refuse the extra tips she might make.

"I at least need a few minutes to sit," she told Ricko.

"Yeah sure," he said from the walk-in refrigerator. "I'll cover your tables for thirty."

Doria grabbed her bag, poured herself a tall glass of iced tea, and headed to the cramped two-seater in the corner. Searching through the never-ending mess that was her bag, she retrieved a bottle of ibuprofen and the sci-fi book she'd grabbed weeks before at the library sale. She hadn't even thought of cracking into it before, but now with a few minutes to herself, she decided it was time to take a peek.

Flipping past the copyright and dedication, she dove into the story.

Jillian and the Tower of Rust

The heavy metal door leading from the living quarters of Quad-base 67A creaked open as Jillian stepped out into the biting cold air of the yard between the tin box she called home and the slightly larger tin box where she worked. She'd been trained to scan the desolate space with her eyes before venturing out across the soft dusty soil, so before going any further, her eyes swept left, right, and back to the left. She knew she needed to stay wary, but just as every other morning, the only things she saw were the dilapidated solar panels jutting out at odd angles and the twin suns rising in the distance. No scurrying sand-mags waiting to rip off a leg and no unrecognized alien intruders. It was as typical a start to the day as she could expect—another in a long chain of endless days, working for just enough to get by.

Jillian sighed, her breath crystallizing in a faintly blue cloud in the air before her. She had a job to do, people relying on her, and a family to feed. She just wished it wasn't so boring. She'd been dreaming of adventure since before she could read, and when the idea of moving to a remote galactic outpost arose, she and her family jumped at the opportunity. Her father accepted the position as maintenance custodian of one of the mining quadrants on a distant dwarf planet. They'd packed up and boarded a transport destined for the little-known corner of the galaxy.

Hypersleep was dangerous. It was a risk she and her parents had understood and taken on for themselves as well as Jillian's younger siblings. Travelers could go under and get ill from the process—bodies breaking down despite the nutrients infused and the oxygen-rich solution they were cocooned in. Death was only one of the risks. Possibly worse than death, the combination could cause one to get trapped within themselves. An endless sleep. It was even part of the paperwork. Travelers had to select if they wanted a swift end at the hands of the med team after a given number of days without waking at their final port.

Jillian's family had all signed the wavers—going for a moderate three week period left in stasis before the final injection was given. They didn't get that time with her mother. She'd died during the transport hypersleep induction and none of them even knew about it until they'd arrived and been woken themselves.

Her mother's death had come as a crushing blow to all of them, but none more so than Jillian's father. Something in him died the day they'd arrived and he was told. He'd withered in front of them and now could do little more than sit up in his bed, leaving Jillian to take on the job intended for him.

The ache in her chest had lessened over time, but it never really left. To add another layer of misery to them all, the outpost was nothing like they'd expected. Her mother would have hated it here as much as the rest of them, but at least she'd be alive.

Jillian shook off the painful thoughts, steeling herself for the hours of work she had in front of her. There were mouths to feed and bills to pay. No time for self-pity.

Trudging through the greenish-grey powdery soil, Jillian made her way across the yard and to the far door leading to the Quad-base proper. She punched in her controller pin and listened as the mechanism inside the door whirred and clicked. With a hiss, the lock popped, and Jillian pulled the door open. Once inside, she resealed the lock and punched the com button on the rusted metal wall. A nauseating yellow glow filled the space and the COM speakers crackled.

"Quad-base 67A prepared to receive com from Galileo Prime." Jillian spoke the same words into the empty room each morning. Sometimes a reply came within moments from the main overstation, but just as often Jillian would wait

an hour or more to hear the voice on the other end. That morning, she was in luck and the speaker clicked and static filled the space just as she was settling in at the control panel.

"Galileo Prime responding to Quad-base 67A. How's it going, Jillian?" A deep male voice asked. It carried a faint accent. One she was sure she'd heard before but couldn't quite place. Off-planet maybe? Jillian leaned forward, warmth flooding her at the sound.

She had never met the man attached to that voice, but Jillian had built an image of him in her mind—strong chiseled jaw, piercing green eyes, and soft brown hair that curled around his ears and at the collar of his uniform. In reality, she knew he could be old and grey with pock-marked skin and a hideous little rat mustache. She preferred her vision of him though.

"I'm good Hank. Just reporting for duty." She chuckled to herself at the man's name. Hank also happened to be the name of her first love, a floppy-eared stuffed bunny she'd carried with her from her toddler years, right through to her teen years when her father convinced her to let Pira start caring for the old toy.

"Got it. Jillian Everhart on duty," came back the over the com. "Try to stay out of trouble today, Jillian. We've been told there might be some seismic activity. Stay alert."

"Will do. Thanks. Com out." She leaned back into her chair with a sigh. There'd been more and more little tremors over the last few weeks. Nothing dangerous, but the increasing frequency made Jillian wonder if something was going on in the mines. If there were, she and her family would just have to ride it out. She wasn't getting paid to worry about tremors anyway. She was getting paid to keep the station up and running.

Let the day's drudgery begin.

By the time she finished with all the maintenance and routine systems runs, she had just enough time to check the security cameras and submit her logs for the month. She included a supply order and requests for her family's personal needs. Those items all came out of her pay, but she didn't want to miss delivery of any of the medication needed to keep her father going, nor any of the little things that kept her younger siblings happy. They were suffering just as much as anyone, stuck inside all day doing virtual education modules on the run-down computer setup. The twins were bundles of energy and would love to be out running the streets of the outpost if it were safe. But it wasn't safe. Not in the least. Jillian didn't like them going outside without someone to watch over them and in the recent months, their father just hadn't been up to it. Jillian always got them out when she was off work, but her shifts were long, and the temperature dropped quickly as soon as the planet turned away from the suns.

She locked up the station and headed back across the yard. She could hear Pira and Oli through the vents before she'd even cracked the exterior door. It sounded like a game of hide and seek. Pretty tough to hide for long in the tiny apartment, but they made it work.

Oli bounded into her as soon as the door opened. She gave him a quick hug before looking around for Pira. "She's hiding in the ration cabinet," Oli said without preamble.

"No fair," Pira yelled as she extricated herself from the tight space.

"You hide there every time," her brother said exasperatedly.

"Not like there's anywhere else to hide," she replied.

"How was your day?" Jillian asked as she retrieved food rations from the cabinet Pira had so recently evacuated. "Learn anything new?"

"Nope nope nopity nope," Oli sang.

"I learned that there is a new hole in the roof outside the bunks," Pira said.

"No," Jillian groaned. "Is there?"

"Yep yep yepity yep," Oli sang again.

The ceiling was already leaking in three other places, creating permanent green puddles where the off-color soil mixed with the rainwater that leaked in.

As the rations heated in the air oven, Jillian began mopping up as best she could. The mop had seen better days. Just as she was finishing up, the lights flickered, then went out entirely. It was the third fuse to blow this week. The place was falling apart around them, but Galileo Prime didn't seem to care. There weren't any permanent maintenance crews assigned this far out and if she wanted the materials to fix it herself, they would eventually send them, but at a hit to her pay. Given how pricey her father's meds were, she just couldn't find a way to pay for both.

After the kids were fed, she led them out into the yard for a few minutes of outside time. Again, she scanned the area before letting them run amuck. Still nothing dangerous, but the clips she'd seen on the news over the last several months made it sound as if no one was safe. Native life on the planet was hostile and she couldn't blame the creepy critters for wanting their habitats back. They had no real right to be there but the rich stores of minerals that had brought humans there decades ago, were just too good to pass up apparently.

Watching her siblings running made Jillian long for just a fraction of their energy. She was tired all the time. And hungry. And restless.

She would give anything for a few days off from the monotony of her current situation. Some days it felt as if she was staggering through life, half asleep.

Doria could relate. She'd felt the same way nearly every day until she'd stumbled into Vespertine Books and met Miles. He'd awoken something in her and brought a fresh new challenge to her life. As much as she hated it, thinking along those lines felt incredibly selfish. He was the one trapped in the same endless space and time.

Thoughts of time had her checking her watch. *Time* for her to get back to work.

With a sigh, she put a battered sticky note in as a bookmark and stowed the paperback back in her bag.

Such a bummer. She was really into the story so far.

The night ended with Doria stuffing a little extra cash into her bag and packing up a carton of chicken potpie to eat when she got home.

She took what she'd come to think of as "her normal route" home. It wasn't a direct shot, but it took her past all the places she thought the bookshop was likely to appear.

Not a sign of it, yet again.

She grabbed a fork, dug into her dinner, and started reading again.

As the suns went down, the first tremor hit. It was larger than the previous ones—a jarring rolling shake that nearly sent her sprawling. Oli whooped and ran an extra lap, arms raised and swinging above his head as the ground settled, but Pira ran straight for Jillian and wrapped her arms around her sister's waist.

She hustled the kids inside and checked on her father. He refused to drink any of the broth she'd made him and barely woke from sleep long enough to thank her for taking care of the twins. It hurt deeply to see him in such a state. The doctors said it was some sort of side effect of the hypersleep. A similar yet less severe form of what had killed her mother, but Jillian had her doubts. To her, it simply looked like he was dying of a broken heart.

Exhaustion tugged at her as she made her way to her bunk. The mattress was lumpy and the blankets scratchy and thin. For the hundredth time, she tried to think of a way to get them out of this place. She needed to save up some money to pay for passage back to Galileo Prime, but with the mounting expenses, she just didn't think it was possible. Still, she refused to give up. If she did, she wouldn't be the only one to suffer.

The supplies were in at the loading depot and that meant Jillian would get a break from the monotony of her job for one whole afternoon. She was required to leave the confines of her life in order to retrieve the cart, drive it back to Quad-base 67A, unload it, and then return the empty cart. The entire process would take most of the day. Because she'd be on foot for a good portion of it, she was required to strap on not only a plasma taser but also a rather barbaric looking knife. They gave her a certain sense of safety, but she knew if something really big and mean came for her, there wasn't much she could do about it.

Things went fairly smoothly and she was happy to see her father's medication in one of the trunks alongside some new book disks for the kids, software updates for their school program, and even the box of hard sugar sweets she'd ordered as a surprise for the twins. The extra fuses, solar panels, and food rations were there as well. It took her no time at all to unload and head back to the depot. She'd just returned the cart and was making her way back home as the suns dipped below the horizon bathing things in an eerie orange glow.

Scuffling from ahead drew her attention and she pulled the taser from its sheath. A man stepped out of the shadows, blocking her path and she froze. Twilight in the thin atmosphere played tricks with his features, making it tough for Jillian to immediately identify him. She raised the taser straight out in front of her and he chuckled.

"There's no need for that Everheart."

Clearly, he knew her, even if she didn't immediately recognize him. "Not here to do you any harm."

Her grip on the plasma taser tightened. "Then what do you want?"

He took a step forward and for the first time, she could make out his face. Piercing blue eyes, a hooked nose, a long burn scar up one side of his neck and face, along with a bitter amusement in his expression identified him as Flet Eo. She knew him only vaguely, but he was hard to miss.

"I want to help you get off this rock."

"Who says I want off?"

He raised one eyebrow. "You telling me you don't?"

"Maybe. But even if I did, unless you've got some hidden stash of flight vouchers or a pile of credit chips, I doubt you could give me a hand."

"It's not credits. But it is a way out."

"What kind of a way?" She couldn't pretend she wasn't interested.

"A private class transport pod. Tomorrow night."

"I can't leave my family."

He nodded as if he expected as much. "There's room for all four of you. Though getting your old man to the site might take some work."

"And why would I trust you?" She didn't trust anyone on this star forsaken rock.

"Let's just say I hate to see a pretty thing like you waste away in a hellhole like this."

Jillian just stared at him, torn between suspicion and hope. "I don't buy it? What do you get out of the deal?"

"I'm sure payment of some sort could be worked out." He smiled as she stepped backward, ready to run.

"Easy, easy." He laughed at her discomfort. "I'll take the taser. You won't be needing it any longer if you get out of here, right?"

Jillian's thoughts raced. A chance at freedom from this miserable place, but at what cost? She looked for any sign of deception in his face, but the truth was she'd have no way to know if he was playing her in some way. After wishing for this very thing for so long, she wasn't sure how she could turn it down. She had to take the risk if only for Pira and Oli's sake. She turned the taser off and handed it to him. "What do I have to do?"

He tossed her a single copper keycard. "Be at the top of the north guard tower tomorrow night at 00:15. Look for the pod Jupiter's Eye and the ugly bastard running it. He'll be expecting you."

She looked down at the key card and nodded.

A slow smile spread across Flet Eo's face. "Excellent. A new life awaits you Jillian Everheart." He tipped his head and walked away back into the shadows.

The key card felt like a tiny burning flame in her hand as she raced home. For the first since she'd woken from hypersleep five years ago, she had a flicker of hope. Flet Eo said the pod left tomorrow. That gave her one night to get to the tower and make sure it wasn't some sort of a prank and to see how in the stars she was going to make it there with her father in tow.

This isn't bad, Doria thought as she turned the page. It reminded her of all the great science fiction she'd read as a kid. She'd always loved dark foreboding tales of vicious aliens and planetary invasions. Even a dystopian thriller warning against man's inevitable demise could be good as long as the messaging was subtle and not bang you over the head preachy.

The twins were asleep and her father was medicated when Jillian slipped out of the apartment.

The north tower was on the far side of the outpost, isolated from the rest of the sparse buildings by a wide field of nothing but grey-green silty sand and a gigantic slag pile left over from mining done years earlier. Standing away from the hulking monstrosity, Jillian looked to the top, hoping to see some sign of the escape she was desperately hoping for. The tower was dark except for a ring of yellow light coming from what looked like several small windows just below the pinnacle.

The field made Jillian nervous, but she tore off across it just the same. If things went well, she'd be traversing it with her father and younger siblings the next night and without her taser to protect them. Nothing stirred as she ran and she was able to make it to the bottom of the tower unscathed. That was something at least.

A heavy door sat in the smooth metal siding of the tower. Finding the key slot, Jillian slid her copper card through and breathed a sigh of relief as the door clicked open. Metal steps spiraled up from the bottom into utter darkness above. Tilting her head back and squinting up, she cursed at the lack of light but knew she would ascend anyway.

The stairs went on for ages. Despite treading as lightly as she could, each step seemed to echo in the confined space. The higher she climbed, the more her legs burned, but she continued to push on. She needed to see, needed to know before she ever returned here with Pira, Oli, and their father.

Along the way to the top, several landings offered doors to various levels. Flet Eo had instructed her to go to the top, so instead of trying any of them, she just kept climbing. After what seemed like hours, but was probably no more than ten minutes, she emerged at the highest floor. Here too sat a door—windowless and solid. Anything could be waiting on the other side; Jillian was desperate for it to be freedom. She knew of course it might be empty. She wasn't supposed to be there until the following night, but on the off chance it was being prepped, she wanted to see for herself.

Taking a steadying breath, she slid the copper key card into the slot. Just as it had at the base, the door clicked and the lock released. She pushed it tentatively, readying herself to fly down the stairs if danger lurked on the other side. As the heavy hatch swung open, her heart leaped to find a large open hanger with a small landing platform on the far side. A banged-up transport pod perched atop it.

She couldn't help the ridiculous grin that spread across her face, but as she approached the old vessel, the grin faded into a bland look of concern. To say it was merely old was insane. It was clearly incapable of flight. One of the thrusters was damaged beyond recognition and the forward hatch was completely missing.

Maybe this was the wrong ship? Rushing to the side she looked for any indication this was the means Flet Eo had meant. And there it was, barely visible beneath the layer of grime, the flaking orange words. "Jupiter's Eye."

With dawning horror, she realized the truth: this was never meant to be their escape. She had been lied to. But for what purpose?

It was too much. She sank to the floor. The cost of replacing the taser alone would set her back months. Was it worth so much to the vile man that he would trick her so cruelly?

The key dropped from her hand and clattered to the floor, the hollow ring of metal on metal echoing the emptiness in her chest. Wiping her hand angrily across her eyes, she scooped the copper rectangle back up and stood. She could cry later. It was time to get back home to her family.

Taking the stairs down, she stopped at the floor below and stared at the locked hatch there. The place seemed to be deserted and she wondered if maybe the answer to the ruse lay behind one of the other hatches. She placed her hand on the cool metal and took a deep breath before sliding the keycard into the slot. Again, the soft click and the release of a lock.

Even more tentatively, she pushed the door open. Rather than a craft platform, this door opened into a small narrow walkway lit by yellow lighting.

"Hello?" she whispered. If there was someone around, she wanted to know now, while she was still close enough to escape down the stairs.

No answer.

She wasn't sure if she felt relieved or more on edge.

Sensing no one, she began to walk down the corridor, gently trailing her fingers along the smooth wall. With each step she took, the temperature seemed to drop until she felt herself shivering slightly. After roughly twenty yards, the walkway began to curve. She couldn't see around the bend, so slowed her steps as she came upon it. As soon as the corridor made the turn, she noticed doors lining one side of the narrow space.

She approached slowly and was startled when a loud bang echoed from one of the doors further down the line. Swearing softly, she threw a hand over her mouth. The air stilled and fell quiet once more. She approached the first door. It looked sturdier than the one leading onto this floor and as she got nearer, she saw that the top half was almost completely transparent. It appeared to be open air, but she noted the small coils on either side of the frame. Looking through the space she realized it was a cell of sorts. Unoccupied and quiet. Looking down the row, she realized the doors were all the same. At least ten cells in all. Each with an empty window in the door.

She continued walking, wondering who these were supposed to house. Crime at the outpost wasn't unheard of but it was rather rare, and she had never heard of anyone being actually punished for anything.

And if they were to house criminals, where were the guards? She hadn't seen any of those at the outpost either. Her heart pounded as she walked past each empty room, the silence unnerving. She would have expected some type of alarm if she wasn't meant to be there. But—nothing. Only the sound of her footsteps and the ragged breathing trying to keep pace with her heart.

As she approached the fifth door, a flicker of movement caught her eye and she darted back. A figure stood in the center of the cell, partially hidden in shadow, and staring out at her. She froze in her tracks, unsure what to do. The figure made no move toward her and made no sound. In the stillness, she could hear a faint buzzing coming from the window-like opening in the door. It appeared as empty as the others. Raising her hand, she moved to put it through the space.

"Don't." She froze again at the command in his voice. "Unless you'd like to lose a finger or two."

She dropped her hand quickly and rubbed it on her pants leg.

The figure stepped closer and cocked his head at her. "It's a plasma field." His voice was quiet now, but still deep and rich and faintly familiar. He had the same off-planet accent as Hank, her radio liaison from Galileo Prime.

Galileo Prime. Her employer would be extremely disappointed if they knew what she was currently up to. She wasn't even supposed to be there, much less talking with someone who was clearly a prisoner. "I've never seen one before."

He didn't answer just continued to watch her as he took another step forward, bringing him more clearly into the light.

He was massive. Easily a foot taller than her. And very clearly not human.

Humanoid, yes. Human, no.

His skin was a deep fuchsia, dotted with yellow spots. His face, all strong angles and completely expressionless, save for the blazing amber of his overly large eyes. He wore a fitted flight suit but was barefoot. The yellow spots faded to speckles on his feet and Jillian noted the same patterning on his hands.

She swallowed hard, her mouth suddenly dry. She had seen the film stories about aliens on the planet and had encountered a few during her work training. But none of them looked like this one. She would have remembered seeing someone like this.

His huge build radiated a predatory energy, even in the confines of his small cell.

A small voice in the back of her mind told her to leave. She was way out of place here. She ignored the voice and remained rooted to the spot studying the alien prisoner with a mix of fear and curiosity. He was studying her with a look of bored indifference. It was that bored indifference that drew her in. That and the lean muscle hidden beneath the beautiful hue of his skin. She almost thought he was sexy.

Shaking her head, she broke the spell and stepped back. Aliens were not sexy. They were aliens. And this one was clearly dangerous. What other reason could there be for him to be locked away in such a place?

Her movement seemed to snap his attention as well. He gave a subtle shake of his head and turned from the door.

"You should leave this place. It is not for you."

"What's not for me?" She wasn't sure if he meant the tower in general or simply this level.

"Any of this. You should leave this place."

"But what is this? Why are you here?" She asked, stepping toward his cell once again.

He looked over his shoulder at her. "It is a place of traps and I don't want to see one sprung on you Jillian Everheart."

That caught her and she felt truly frightened for the first time since swiping the copper key card. "How do you know my name?" She whispered.

"I know many things," he replied cryptically. "And right now, I know, you are not meant to be here. Although they planned for their procedure tomorrow, it is not to say it won't be sprung early."

It was all a trap. The key card, the escape pod, the offer to get her and her family off this wretched planet. But why? She had nothing worth anything. Her anger and her frustration boiled over. She wasn't leaving until she had some answers.

"No. I won't be leaving just yet." She looked at the door, searching for a key card slot.

"What are you doing?"

He'd turned full forward and was facing her once more. Now instead of bored confusion, he looked worried.

"I'm looking for the lock mechanism."

"Why?"

"So, you can get out of that cell. If someone wants to trap me so badly, then they can deal with me untrapping *someone too."*

"Don't be foolish." His large eyes flashed with irritation and some other emotion she couldn't quite place. "If I wanted to escape, I would have done so already."

That pulled her up short. "You can't mean you want to be imprisoned here?"

"Can't I?" He crossed his well-muscled arms over his chest.

"No. . . I mean. Why would you want that?"

"Traps and plans and breaking procedures." What the hell did that even mean? "Now you really should be going."

"And if I chose not to?" Jillian shot back. She didn't know why exactly she was so determined to stay here and argue. Likely it was due to her hopes being dashed earlier and her frustration with her life. She wanted an adventure and this looked like the closest she would come to it.

He studied her for a moment longer then sighed and ran his hand through his long violet hair in what looked like a very human gesture. "This ridiculous stubbornness will cost us both."

She smiled slightly. Her mother had always said she was stubborn. "At least tell me your name."

He set his lips in a firm line and looked down on her.

"Oh, come on. You know mine. It's fair. Your name and I'll leave."

He thought it over for a moment. "Xyren."

"That's it? Just Xyren?" She studied him a moment then smirked and asked, "You don't by chance know a guy named Hank do you?"

His eyes flashed wide and then he shook his head. "No. And Xyren is enough for now." He stood a moment longer, arms still crossed over his chest and legs slightly apart. "Now go."

Fair was fair. He'd given his name and that had been Jillian's price.

Turning to leave, she pulled up short when he spoke again. "Stop on the last landing at the bottom of the tower. If the door is unguarded, use your keycard to open it. You'll find stacks of credit chips there. No one will notice if one or two go missing."

Was he telling her to steal? She was no thief. Looking back one last time, she hurried down the corridor and away from the cell. As she made it to the door, she turned, but the bend in the walkway made it impossible for her to see anything, much less the window into his cell. Hitting the door, she made sure it closed completely behind her and then took off down the stairs. The descent was easier than the climb, but still, her legs were jelly by the time she reached the bottom.

She didn't take his advice and left the last landing door firmly shut. She needed the money, yes, but she wasn't some common criminal. And perhaps that was the trap itself.

She exited the tower and hauled it across the open expanse of dirt to the safety of the outpost buildings. Only when she was hidden among the shadows did she look up at the rust covered monolith and the ring of yellow lights toward the top. She wondered if Xyren had watched her run from the building and if he had, what he was thinking when he did.

5

JILLIAN yawned widely as she waited for Galileo Prime to respond over the COM system. It was either taking much longer than normal or it just felt that way as she struggled to keep her eyelids open.

She caught herself drifting, chin in her palm, just as the speaker crackled to life.

"Galileo Prime responding to Quad-base 67A. Ms. Everheart, please report." Huh. Odd. The voice on the other end always seemed so friendly and open. It was one of the things she looked forward to each morning. That morning, however, he was all business.

"Uh, yes. This is Quad-base 67A. Jillian Everheart. Just reporting in for duty."

"Noted." There was a click and the com went silent.

Shaking her head, Jillian grabbed the maintenance logs and the small tool kit she needed and set off to check all of the systems in her quadrant of the outpost.

As she worked, she thought about the small adventure she'd had the night before. While her hopes of escape had been dashed, the night had at least provided her with a certain sense of excitement. She'd done something courageous—if not a little foolish—and in the process had discovered Xyren.

She had a hard time keeping her mind off of the tall muscular being. She longed to know what he was being held for and why—if he was to be believed and could escape—he hadn't. She was more than a little preoccupied by the mystery of it all. If she was being honest, it wasn't just that she'd apparently been set up. She couldn't begin to fathom why someone would want to catch her and her family trying to leave the outpost. All sorts of people wanted to leave. They just couldn't afford it. But more than that, it was Xyren himself. He was clearly a prisoner, and highly likely dangerous. But dangerous to who? It didn't seem like he meant her any harm. In fact, she got the strangest sense of connection with him. Did the upper ranks at Galileo Prime catch him doing something illegal? She certainly hadn't heard any recent stories along those lines, but then again, why would she?

The day went by in a blur. Com system check, smooth fuchsia skin. Wiring reroutes, large amber eyes. Drainage valve coupling, plasma field cells. Dust corrosion film, traps set to spring. Temperature control settings, stacks of credit chips. Weather log filing, tall, broad, muscular, tight. . .

She needed to get her head examined. There was absolutely zero reason she should be interested at all in a man who was one, not human, and two, obviously a criminal of some sort.

It was simply he hadn't seemed like a criminal. Well, maybe a criminal. He did tell her to steal some credit chips.

Her experience with the opposite sex was limited, to say the least. The outpost didn't offer a great social scene and even if it did, she was too busy working and keeping her family alive to partake in it. And he had been rather dreamy to look at. That was it. She would blame her preoccupation with the tall alien in the tall tower on a lack of dating and a desperate need to connect with someone.

What she did know, was as much as she wanted to return to the tower and see Xyren again, there was no way she was going to do it that night. Flet Eo had intended for her to be in that tower and if there was a trap ready to spring, she had no intention of being caught in it.

So, she finished up her logs and reports, made the small repairs she could, and signed out for the night. If she were lucky, she'd get some sleep before she had to do it all over again the next day.

When she returned to work the next morning, she was feeling slightly better rested, but still had her mind on things she shouldn't. What had happened the night before when she hadn't arrived as expected? Was Flet Eo himself there and waiting to pounce or was he only an intermediary of sorts? If it wasn't him, then who would have been waiting for her and her family? And more importantly, why did they want her in the first place? Lastly, even though she knew it didn't matter when so many other questions were left unanswered, was Xyren still in his cell and did he hope he would see her again?

"Quad-base 67A prepared to receive com from Galileo Prime."

She barely released the com button when the speaker crackled to life.

"Galileo Prime responding to Quad-base 67A. Jillian is that you?" The male voice was full of both disbelief and not a little excitement.

"It is. Who else would it be?"

"I, uh, no one. I'm just happy to hear you this morning." He seemed to rein in his enthusiasm and asked, "Are you good there?"

"Yep. All good. Just reporting for work."

"Right. Great. Well then, have a good shift. Out."

If she wasn't suspicious before, the difference in interactions between the two days, cemented it in her mind. Jillian needed to know now, more than ever, what was happening at the tower. And there was only one way to find out.

Bustling through her work, she raced home, fed her siblings, checked on her father, and then informed him she was going out for the evening. His initial worry was soon replaced by heavy snores as he drifted off to sleep while she was still in the room.

The guilt she felt at leaving was heavy on her shoulders and she told herself she would abandon her exploration at the first sign of trouble. The last thing she wanted was to get caught and leave her siblings to fend for themselves. But someone had intended to harm her the night before, and now she felt a little less guilty about taking a look at those credit chips. She could slip in, check the door Xyren had suggested, and slip right back out.

She told herself if she was careful, perhaps over time she might get her hands on enough of them to pay for passage off the dwarf planet on a legitimate transport vessel. She told herself it had nothing to do with the sexy alien being held there. It was for her family. For their safety. If the tower was deserted, however, she might just make the climb up and see if Xyren was still being held.

As she raced across the open expanse, gravel and dust crunched beneath her boots. The rusted tower loomed before her, a halo of lights from the uppermost windows. Heart racing, she checked over her shoulder. All was still. She swiped the keycard and slipped inside.

Seeing no one, she hurried up the first flight of stairs to the landing Xyren had mentioned. The place once again appeared to be deserted. She swiped her key card, certain if as many credit chips were there as Xyren claimed, it would flash red and she'd be out of luck. To her surprise, the door hissed and opened. Checking once more she was alone, she hurried inside.

Xyren hadn't lied. The place was filled with not just credit chips, but all sorts of valuable items. Stacks of electronic parts, food rations, and most importantly, weapons filled the space. Not just plasma tasers, but long-range laser rifles, small magnetic grenades, and piles of solar energy whips sat neatly arranged in rows and stacks. Her stomach dropped. For years she'd been asking for some of these things in her monthly acquisition requests only to be denied due to lack of funding. Her siblings weren't starving, but they were hungry more often than not. As she walked further in, something on one of the back shelves caught her eye. Her stomach dropped and fury rose inside her. There, carefully wrapped and labeled, were stacks and stacks of cartons marked with the same "Rx" insignia her father's medications carried.

All this time, the lifesaving medicine he needed was right there, not more than a stone's pitch from where he needed it. And on more than one occasion, she'd watched him suffer as they were told the shipment was delayed.

What in all the cycle of the suns was going on?

As she stood there studying the cartons, the sound of heavy boots on the metal stairs reached her.

Shit. She was not only out of time, she was also trapped here. She needed to get to the door and be ready to run.

Taking Xyren's advice, she grabbed three credit chips and shoved them into her pack. If she was caught, she was in deep no matter if she had the chips or not. Might as well make it worth it if she escaped unscathed.

Standing by the door, she listened for the sounds of footfalls. They were there, all right. And getting closer. Steeling herself, she backed against the wall next to the door. The footstep stopped just outside and to Jillian's utter horror, the sound of a keycard being swiped could be heard. Taking a deep breath, she prepared to make a run for it. Just as the door cracked, a violent tremor hit. The entire tower groaned and creaked with the assault of it. As the ground stilled, whoever was on the other side of the door, ran off shouting about checking for damage.

Jillian gave it to the count of thirty before she cracked the door and peered outside. The landing was clear, but she could still hear voices from down below at the tower's base level entry. Not sure what else to do, she made her way up the stairs until she arrived once more on the level full of cells.

Rounding the bend toward Xyren's cell, she ran smack into a solid wall of grey clad muscle. She would have gone down if not for the fuchsia and gold speckled hands that grabbed her arms and held her upright.

"What are you doing here?" the tall alien hissed at her. "I thought I told you this place was a trap."

Rather than answer him, Jillian asked a question of her own. "Why are you out of your cell?"

"I told you I could leave whenever I wanted," he responded. "Plus, the turbulence always messes with the power. The plasma shields will be down for a few minutes."

"Turbulence? You mean the seismic activity?"

He looked momentarily confused, then nodded. "Yes. Sorry. I meant the tremors."

He looked down the corridor and shook his head. "You really shouldn't be here. It's time to go."

"But what is this place?" she demanded. "I stopped in the room you mentioned on my way up here. It's loaded with all sorts of stuff. Not just the credit chips."

He grabbed her elbow gently and led her back toward the stairs. "I told you before. It's all one big trap. Take the credit chips and go. Go and don't come back."

"I'm not going anywhere until I get some answers. Why would anyone want to trap me or my family here? What have we done to warrant that?"

"Sometimes you don't have to do anything to warrant a cruel punishment. It's just the way of the universe." He stopped when they reached the landing. "The guards should be gone by now. They never stay around too long. Head home and promise me you'll stay there." His large amber eyes were beseeching—looking for a promise she couldn't give. "If anyone asks you to return, flat refuse."

When she stayed silent, he sighed and ran a hand through his hair. He studied her face for a heartbeat. "Your stubbornness will be your undoing Jillian Everheart."

"Perhaps," she conceded. "But anything has to be better than this half-existence I've been living."

His expression softened. The atmosphere between them shifted. A spark of understanding flashed in his eyes. It was that spark that helped push her toward trust. Jillian knew Xyren must be dangerous, but she sensed he meant her no direct harm. The pull she felt toward him went beyond physical attraction. It was a kinship born from nothing more than random coincidence. He was here in the tower and she wanted to uncover how it related to her and her family. Even though he claimed he could leave whenever he liked, she didn't believe him. She would help him escape.

Without thinking, she raised on her toes and placed her hands on his smooth skin. "I am going to keep coming back here until we get you out. I don't care how long it takes."

He frowned at her words, sadness filling his eyes. "I'm not willing to become part of your downfall Jillian. I'm not meant to add to the snare."

"Don't worry. I won't be easily caught."

"I'm afraid you already are." He barely whispered the words before his mouth was crushing down onto hers. His lips were soft and commanding and Jillian welcomed each blissful stroke and tug. The kiss was brief but so full of longing, Jillian nearly went weak in the knees.

As Xyren pulled back, he looked at her with eyes full of remorse. "I shouldn't have done that. You don't need another reason to return to this place. Time is running out. The shields will be up again soon and I need to return before they do. Go, Jillian. Please."

She nodded. "I'll be back for you. I promise."

He shook his head in defeat before turning and walking back to his cell.

In the week that followed, Jillian continued to work during the day, care for family in the evening, and take just enough time to race to the tower to steal a few more chips and to see Xyren each night. On two occasions, she even managed to swipe extra medication vials for her father.

Every morning Hank checked in on her over the radio com. His voice seemed to get more pinched, his accent thicker, each time they spoke. He was concerned. That much was obvious. She just wasn't sure why. She didn't think he could possibly know about her nightly trips to the tower. Perhaps it was due to the increase in tremors occurring daily. When before they'd been only every few weeks, the rolling quakes were now happening daily and they seemed to be getting stronger.

Each night when she made it to the tower, Xyren too seemed more and more agitated. Some nights she would make it to his cell to find the plasma shield off and others he would meet her on the landing or the stairs. While she knew he was frustrated that she kept returning, it didn't stop him from crushing her to his chest and kissing her with a ravenous hunger she couldn't explain. They'd only just met, but he seemed as desperate for her as she did for him.

Each visit got shorter and shorter, with him insisting she leave before the trap was sprung. Each time she'd ask what sort of trap he was referring to. She hadn't seen any further signs of guards or other indications of impending doom. In fact, Xyren seemed to be the only other living soul in the entirety of the tower. She was starting to worry he was staying there on purpose, not a prisoner at all. He insisted he couldn't explain the sort of trap ready to spring, but repeatedly told her to take the credit chips she collected each night and book passage off the outpost. She'd collected enough and while she wanted nothing more than to get her father and siblings away from the desolate place, she refused to go without Xyren.

"It doesn't work that way, Jillian," he insisted for the dozenth time. "I can't just leave with you."

When she'd arrived that night, the plasma shield was up and Xyren sat on the bench at the far side of his cell. He wore only his grey flight trousers, his chest bare and muscular. In the dim light, she could make out the intricate patterns the golden spots made over his torso. She wanted desperately to run her hands over his muscled chest and arms.

"I don't understand why not. You won't tell me anything. You won't explain anything." She paced in front of his door, frustration, and longing mixing into a violent conflagration beneath her skin. "It's like I'm trapped in this cycle without knowing how to break it."

He looked at her with his mysterious amber eyes, a heartbreaking frown on his beautiful face. "You're closer now to figuring it out." He said cryptically then he stood and mirrored her pacing on his side of the door. "I want you to leave and not come back. If you can do that for me, I promise to find you wherever you go."

Something tickled in the back of Jillian's brain, but no matter how hard she tried, she couldn't get it to settle into focus.

"What if you can't?" She felt tears threatening behind her eyes.

"I will. I promise. There is nowhere out there you could go that I wouldn't find you."

She wanted to believe his words. Wanted to leave this place with her family. Wanted to break free from the outpost. The tower. Her life.

"I can't leave like this. Not with you stuck on that side of the door." Just as the words left her mouth, another tremor hit, this one even more violent than the others. The tower vibrated with its intensity. Jillian stumbled back as the metal groaned and shrieked around her. Then the plasma shield went down and she was running toward Xyren.

She crossed the space on shaking legs and ran her hands over the velvety softness of his skin. He was so alien and yet so achingly familiar to her. A silent question passed between them.

"You are so beautiful, Jillian. I shouldn't want this with you. The guilt is eating me up." His normally clipped accent was even thicker now.

"There's nothing to feel guilty about. I want this Xyren. I want you." She nuzzled in closer to him, inhaling his scent and trailing her hands over every exposed inch of him.

His lips crashed into hers, hot and demanding. His hands fisted in her hair as he pulled her tighter against the hard planes of his body. Jillian pulled back just long enough to grab the hems of her shirt, then tugged it up over her head and tossed it aside. Her athletic bra followed close behind it. Xyren's eyes drank her in before he tentatively ran his palms over her bare breasts and Jillian shivered at the warmth in his hands on her body. She'd spent days aching for his touch and now, in this prison cell, she finally had it.

She arched into him and Xyren ran a trail of searing kisses down her neck to her collarbone. She arched into him, moaning softly as the evidence of his desire pressed into her. His thumb glided over her nipple and he rolled it between his fingers before lowering his head further. Jillian gasped as his mouth closed over her breast. His lips and tongue worked slow delicious magic, teasing, and stroking as her desire for him grew and grew. Heat coiled through her and she rocked her hips against his thigh instinctively.

A growl rumbled in Xyren's chest as he switched to her other breast, kneading, and suckling until she was trembling in his arms. Only then did he raise his head, eyes glowing with lust.

There were so many reasons this was wrong. So many ways it could end in disaster. But in the moment, with Xyren's lips and hands moving over her fevered skin, none of it mattered. All that existed was this cell. This tower. This alien who had somehow become so important to her. The passion between them threatened to consume her.

Another terrifying tremor rocked the tower. The lights flicked and a panel fell from overhead. Metal groaned and Xyren pulled away gasping. The flush of lust was still there, but it was covered with another stronger emotion. Jillian thought it might be shame. "Fuck," he breathed.

He reached down and snatched up Jillian's bra and shirt. "I'm so sorry Jillian. This isn't right. We can't do this. I can't do this. Get dressed and get out of here."

Did she just imagine the connection burning between them? "But—" she started to argue, just as another quake hit.

"Don't argue this time. Just go." His tone was biting. "Get your family on the next transport out."

"What about you?"

"I meant what I said. I'll find you." She should have been happy with his words, but it sounded more like a dismissal.

"I want you to come with me." She wasn't beyond begging at this point.

"I can't. And Jillian?" She looked up into his large amber eyes. "Don't come back again. I mean it this time. I won't be here waiting for you if you."

His words felt like a slap to the face after what had just happened. What they'd almost done. She felt rejected and diminished. Tears of humiliation stung her eyes as she raced down the steps. The tower continued to shake and vibrate as repeated aftershocks rocked the ground beneath it.

As she raced home, she saw others in the settlement collecting up their things and heading to the transport hub. She knew then things were bad. It looked as if the entire outpost was evacuating.

A wave of guilt crashed into her. She should have been home packing up Oli and Pira, her father and his medications, not throwing herself at an alien prisoner who didn't want her.

She made it to the apartment and flew through the door as the shaking intensified.

"Jillian," Oli threw himself at her. Pira was right behind him. "What's happening?"

"We need to get out of here and to the transport hub," she said in a breathless wheeze. "Get your packs. I'll get Dad and his medications."

She raced to her bunk and shoved aside the mattress to retrieve the small hoard of credit chips she'd been accumulating. She scooped them into her pack along with her father's last few doses of medicine before strapping on her knife.

"What about our toys?" Pira asked.

"Leave them. We'll get you some new things when we get out of here." Jillian raced into her father's room to find him sitting up in bed. "Come on Dad. It's time to go."

"Oh, honey. I don't think I can. Take the kids and get out of here."

"No. We aren't doing that. Come on. I'll help you." She bent down and pulled her father's arm around her neck, wrapping her free arm around his waist. "Oli, do you think you can carry my pack too?"

Her brother nodded and hefted the strap across his thin shoulders, wearing her pack in the front and his on his back. He grabbed Pira's hand and they trudged out into the night.

"What if there are sand-mags out here?" Jillian's sister asked in a small voice.

"There won't be," Jillian reassured her. "But if there are, I'll take care of them."

Off in the distance, she could make out the lights of transport pods lifting off from the hub. She hoped she wasn't too late. She would never forgive herself if she'd sacrificed her family's safety all because she had gotten inexplicably attached to Xyren.

The walk took longer than it should have. Jillian was beyond exhausted and her body just didn't want to do the things she was asking of it. She'd been undernourished and overworked for weeks now. Adding in the recent nights of little to no sleep and she was little more than a walking shell. Despite all of it, she was practically carrying her father by the time they arrived.

There was just one transport left in the hangar. Jillian dropped the credit chips on the counter and a harried older man took them without looking up. "Get on then," he instructed.

Jillian's relief was all-consuming as she settled her father, Pira, and Oli into open seats and fastened all their flight buckles. Dropping into the open spot next to Pira, she glanced out the window just as the massive metal tower in the distance came crashing down.

Her heart clenched as she watched the metal fold over on itself and slam into the open space, she'd raced across so many times recently. A plume of silt and dust rose into the air and Jillian couldn't suppress a sob as she thought about Xyren. Had he been in the tower as it fell? She told herself he wasn't. He'd said he could escape at any time and had told her he wouldn't be there waiting for her again. With any luck, he had been true to his word and was on one of the other transports fleeing the outpost.

She hadn't bothered to ask where the pod was taking them. She would figure it all out when they got there. With any luck, it would be somewhere warm and safe. With even more luck, they'd have a doctor to tend to her father. She didn't dare to hope Xyren would be there waiting for her.

She watched out the window as their craft lifted off. Silent tears streamed down her cheeks as the dwarf planet grew smaller and smaller. Soon it was nothing more than a distant pinprick of light.

She was weary to her very bones. Glancing at her father and siblings, she saw they were all dosing in their respective seats. Her body was telling her she should do the same. Get some rest while she could. Who knew what would be thrown at them next?

Eventually, her eyes drifted closed and she fell into a dark and dreamless sleep.

Jillian could hear the soft whirs and beeps of machinery as she fought to the surface of her slumber. The pings sounded familiar but different from the noises she'd drifted off to on their escape from the outpost.

The outpost. The tower. Xyren.

She hadn't even opened her eyes yet and still, she wanted to squinch them shut against the memory.

The beeping noise began to pick up tempo.

From far away she heard someone call out. "She's waking up. I think she'd waking up." The woman's voice sounded so much like her mother. But that couldn't be right. Her mother was dead. A victim of the hypersleep sickness that had almost taken her father as well.

"Are you sure?" That was definitely her father's voice.

"She's been murmuring and I know I just saw her move her hands. Then her eyes fluttered," the woman who sounded like her mother said. "Do you think it worked?"

"I certainly hope so." A clipped and accented deep male voice answered. Xyren? Or Hank? They sounded so similar. But why would either of them be here on her transport pod?

"Jillian. Can you open your eyes for me?" All business and concern. Hank then. "Come on now, wake up."

Jillian's eyes fluttered open and immediately she shut them against the bright and blinding light shining overhead.

"There you go. Let me see those beautiful eyes." Maybe Xyren after all?

Her lids were ten-pound weights sitting over her eyes. It took every ounce of energy she had to merely pull them open.

"There you are." The voice said. "Oh, thank all that is good in the universe. There you are, Jillian."

She could hear the woman who sounded like her mother weeping not far off. She was being comforted by the someone who sounded like her father.

Her eyes were hazy and blurred. Her vision filled with a lovely shade of fuchsia. She blinked several times and the fuchsia resolved into a face set with gorgeous amber oversized eyes and framed by violet hair. He was here with her and just as handsome as he'd been when she left him on the outpost.

"Xyren?" she croaked.

He nodded. "I'm here Jillian. Right here."

"But you were in the tower. I saw it fall."

"I got out before you brought it down."

She was muddled and confused. She hadn't brought anything down. She'd escaped with her family just in time.

She tried to shake her head, but it sent a wave of nausea through her.

"No, she whispered. It wasn't me. It was the seismic activity. The mines I think."

"It was you, Jillian. You did it. You escaped the snare." He brought his hand to her face and stroked a thumb over her cheek. "I'll explain it all later. Right now, there are some people who very much want to see you."

She made to grab his hand. She didn't want to lose him again. Not after all that had happened.

"I'll be right here." He held her hand but stepped to the side to make room for the crying woman and the man who might be her father.

"Oh, sweet girl," the woman dropped to the bed beside Jillian and clutched her arm sobbing. "We thought we lost you."

"Mom?" Jillian couldn't make sense of what was happening. "How are you here?"

"I've been here the whole time."

What the actual hell? This was a straight up Wizard of Oz, Aunt Em plot twist and Doria had not seen it coming at all.

Jillian looked past her mother's huddled form to her father—strong and well and whole. "Dad? You aren't sick anymore?"

"I haven't been sick honey? We woke up from the hypersleep just fine. Your brother and sister too. You've been out for weeks though. We didn't think we'd get you back," her father's voice was thick with emotion. "We made it here to Galileo Prime. It's beautiful. I can't wait for you to see the gleaming city."

"Galileo Prime? Not on the outpost?"

"What outpost?" her mother asked through the lump in her voice. "We're on Galileo Prime. The move remember?"

Jillian's brain was in a fog. She didn't remember. She shook her head.

"I think she needs a little time," Xyren explained to her parents. "Most people trapped in hypersleep never make it out. Her body needs time to adjust."

"What do you mean trapped in hypersleep?" She looked up at him.

"You didn't wake up when we docked." Her father answered. "The doctors thought you were gone. We were getting close to the three week limit. I can't believe we signed off on such a short time period. It's only thanks to this young man that you're awake at all."

"I was trapped in hypersleep?"

"You should leave this place. It is not for you."

"What's not for me?"

"Any of this. You should leave this place."

"But what is this? Why are you here?" She asked, stepping toward his cell once again.

He looked over his shoulder at her. "It is a place of traps and I don't want to see one sprung on you Jillian Everheart."

Her initial conversation with Xyren came back to her.

"But—" she blinked again trying to clear her brain. "It was all so real. You were there with me." She looked at her parents and then again at Xyren.

"He thought he could get you out and he did." Her father beamed at Xyren.

"It wasn't real?" Jillian looked helplessly at Xyren. "Who even are you then?"

A wave of nausea rolled through her. Whether it was the effects of her condition or the memory of what she thought she'd shared with Xyren she couldn't say.

"Maybe you could give me a moment alone with Jillian?" he asked her parents. "I think this might be all a little overwhelming."

Her mother looked reluctant, but at the urging of her father, she relented. Jillian was left alone with the beautiful alien man she felt she knew but clearly didn't.

"I'm sure you're very confused." He wore the same remorseful expression she'd seen on him when he was trying to push her away in the tower. "Let me try to explain."

She nodded silently.

"When you and your family arrived here on Galileo Prime, we couldn't get you to wake from your hypersleep. Normally it's a death sentence." He looked miserable as he spoke.

Jillian held up a hand. "Wait. Before you go on. We haven't actually met, have we? Who are you exactly?"

He smiled in a self-deprecating way. "Sorry. Yes, that is probably the best place to start. My name is Xyren. But you knew me in your dream as both Xyren and Hank."

"They were both you?"

"*Right. I'm one of the staff physicians here on site. It was my job to monitor you as you woke. When you heard my voice as Hank, it was just me checking in and monitoring you as you were coming out of hypersleep. We have a protocol to use a benign comforting name so as not to cause stress to the sleeper. Your paperwork indicated Hank was. . .*"

"*My childhood stuffed toy,*" she answered for him.

He smiled in acknowledgment. "*But then all of a sudden you stopped responding and your wake cycling was going offline. I tried to keep tabs on you, but you kept getting deeper and deeper. I knew you were in trouble. I've seen it happen a handful of times, but never to someone so young and strong as you appeared to be.*" He took a deep breath. "*I couldn't just let you stay there. Trapped in your own mind. The only thing I could think of was to try to get to your subconscious and convince you to come out on your own. I didn't have any idea what I was doing but I tapped into you anyway. I'm sorry for that, but I couldn't think of anything else to try.*"

"*But you were there. In the tower.*"

"*The tower was your mind. In your dream state, you constructed a world to live in and somehow convinced yourself to go to the tower. The first time you went there, was just days before your three week contract. We were going to have to administer the meds that would end your stasis. I believe you would have died if you'd stayed as you intended.*"

"*Flet Eo was my mind's way of knowing I was going to die?*"

He shrugged. "*Perhaps. It's tough to say. The tower was just a construct. I had to convince you to leave but that proved harder than I anticipated.*"

"*Because you were there!*" she nearly yelled at him. "*I wanted to stay there because you were there. And all that time none of it was real. Oh, no.*" Jillian felt nauseous again.

"Do you know what I dreamt about? Do you know why I kept going back?"

Xyren hung his head. "Yes." His voice was small and full of shame.

"And you just let me keep returning? Why didn't you tell me?"

"I couldn't tell you. The mind is very fragile. If I had told you it was all just a dream, it could have been catastrophic for you." His already beautiful skin flushed a deeper more violet hue. "Believe me. I knew what I was doing was wrong, but I couldn't stay away either. I kept trying to prod you in the right direction. To get you to leave and not return. I needed you to do that on your own."

"So, you were there, in my mind, sharing all of those conversations with me. Sharing all those actions with me?" She was mortified now.

"I was. Not physically, but mentally. And thank all the stars in the universe I was smart enough to make sure I was alone whenever I tapped into your thoughts. My mind was there but my body was here. If anyone had walked in to see my reactions to you, well, it would have been the end of my attempts to save you. Those kinds of relationships are frowned upon."

While she could certainly imagine why, she asked instead, "Because we aren't both human?"

"No. Because you were technically my patient." He blew out a long breath and ran a hand through his hair. "I'm sorry I let things go as far as I did between us Jillian. I understand if you are disgusted by me. I just needed you to wake up, but even that is no excuse. You deserved better."

"But it worked, didn't it? Without you convincing me to take the credit chips, I never would have been able to pay for the transport and the place was collapsing all around us."

"Those tremors were your body's way of telling you it was failing. You woke up just in time. If you had listened the first time I told you to leave, it would have been so much easier. I still don't understand why you kept coming back."

"I kept coming back for you. But in the end, it didn't matter. None of it was real." Jillian felt the tears overflowing her eyes. She put her face in her hands and blocked him from her sight. She had thought there was a connection to the beautiful man stuck high in the tower. But the connection was one of her own mind's making. She was humiliated and heartbroken all at once.

"It was all real Jillian. That's what I'm saying. I could have stopped showing up in that tower, but in truth, I wanted to see you and talk to you just as much as you wanted to see me. I could have realized what was happening sooner, but I wanted to feel your mouth on mine. I could have pushed you away and told you I wouldn't be there, but I was selfish and scared. I fell for you just like you fell for me. Just because it was in your dreaming state doesn't mean I wasn't wide awake and aware of everything I was doing." He stood and walked to the door. "I'm glad you're awake. I'll have one of the other physicians see to your care moving forward. You should be released to go on with your new life in the next day or two."

"What if I don't want another physician?" She asked.

"You have no say in the matter I'm afraid." He gave her a sad smile. "Let your brain wake up and I'm sure you'll be happy to be in someone else's hands."

"I don't think I will."

"Your stubbornness will be your undoing Jillian."

"I've been told that before."

He tipped his head and exited the room, sending her parents rushing back in.

Jillian was released from the med unit two days later. She didn't see Xyren at all during that time.

Her parents had a beautiful apartment overlooking the park. Taking Oli and Pira to the playground was one of her favorite things in all the universe to do.

Over the next few weeks, her brain fog cleared and her memories came fully back—not just from before she went into hypersleep, but those from her dream state too. While Xyren had felt remorseful about his part in getting her to wake, she felt no such doubts. She understood what he'd meant about it being real, even if it were only in her mind. She'd come to know him in that in-between place and as much as it seemed impossible, she missed him.

That was how she came to be standing outside the med unit one balmy afternoon as Xyren was leaving the building. She stepped into his path and extended a hand.

"Hello. My name is Jillian Everheart. Would you care to grab a drink?"

Doria blew out a long breath and she shut the book. The story was a wild one for sure and while part of her was disgusted by the idea of a person in a position of power acting on his desire, she was also blown away by how the story twisted up at the end. It wasn't what she had been expecting and she was kind of a fan of that.

As she cleaned up her dinner, one thought kept coming back to her. Jillian had been dreaming but that didn't mean the connection between her and Xyren was any less real. Because for him, it had been real. He'd been conscious and awake and driving the interaction. Jillian's mind too had played a part in their connection. She decided to keep returning.

Doria was well aware of the mind-body connection, but she'd never thought of it in those terms before. While this was just a bit of light fiction, maybe it held an important key to her current situation.

Now more excited than ever to go to sleep, she showered quickly and snuggled into her bed. If she was right, Miles might just be waiting for her again in her dreams.

6

HER eyes had barely closed before they flew wide and alert once more. Despite being in her bed, Doria knew in the muddled and watery way of half-lucid thoughts, she was dreaming.

She popped out of bed, no longer in the soft pajamas she'd put on after her shower, but in leggings and a sports bra. Without a second thought, she sprinted out into the night.

As she turned the corner, she saw autumn pumpkins and Halloween décor coating the buildings of the town. It was still the throws of summer, but her dream didn't care. As she crossed the street, her shabby neighborhood flickered, and by the time she stepped onto the adjacent sidewalk, she was standing next to the used appliance store. Another blink and the bookshop's glass door flickered into existence directly in front of her.

Pushing open the door, she wasn't met by either a bell or a gong, but rather by the loud crowing of an overexcited rooster.

The door hadn't fully shut before she was crushed against Miles' chest.

"You're here." He kissed her forehead, then her nose, each of her eyelids, and finally his lips settled on hers. "How long?" he demanded.

"Weeks again." Her voice hitched on the words. "It's been weeks."

The rush of his breath against the top of her head had her heart cracking for him once more.

"It doesn't matter," he said. "You're here now."

Doria wasn't sure who he was trying to convince. Himself or her.

"Miles, I have so much to tell you." She wrapped her arms around his waist and buried her face in the warm welcoming scent of him. "I know this is just a dream, but I think I've finally figured some things out."

He pulled back just enough to turn and grasp her hand, pulling her over to the sofa. Doria noticed with a smile, her favorite chair was once again back in its place. It didn't matter that the soft velvet had been replaced with a ridiculous gold brocade cushion and was accompanied by a similarly covered footstool.

Miles dragged her down next to him and placed an overlarge glass of wine in her hand. She could practically bathe in the thing.

"If I drink all of that, I'll be drunk in no time," she said.

"I don't think you can get drunk in a dream," he replied.

She thought on it and shrugged before taking an enormous gulp. "You're probably right."

He fiddled with a lock of her hair as he studied her face. "I've missed you."

She nodded. "Me too. But that's part of what I wanted to tell you. I read the most amazing book last night and—"

He cut her off. "We don't always have to talk about just books Doria. I haven't seen you in weeks. I haven't seen anyone in weeks."

"I know." She leaned forward and pressed a kiss to his lips. "I didn't want to discuss the book—it probably wouldn't have been to your liking anyway—but it gave me the idea about coming here. How to see you more often."

"Oh?"

"Yeah. It was an odd little science fiction genre mash-up and it made me realize that while I'd prefer you in my waking arms, seeing you in my dreams doesn't have to be any less real. So, when I went to sleep tonight, I just told myself I would dream about you and I hoped somehow the crazy connection I have with the shop would make sure you were here waiting for me. It looks like it worked." She was so giddy, she could hardly contain herself. Giddy was not a feeling she was used to.

Miles seemed to realize how invested she was in the idea and pulled her in for another kiss. "So," he said after he'd just about driven her wild with need, "you think you can show up here every night then?"

She was flushed and warm when she answered. "I don't honestly know, but I'm willing to give it a try."

"Good. Because I've been a wreck since I saw you last."

"I doubt very much you have ever been a wreck in your entire life," Doria teased.

"There have been some days, I can assure you. Having you yanked away just as things were *escalating* last time, was a bit on the rough side."

"Well then, let's *escalate* them again." Doria stood and snapped her fingers. Instantly she was standing before him in nothing but a black lacy thong.

Miles grunted as if he'd been punched in the gut.

Doria smiled down at him. "That was easier than I thought," she mused.

He reached out and wrapped his hands around the back of her thighs and pulled her body close until she had to spread her feet wide or risk toppling over his knees.

Miles kissed her just below the belly button as he continued to stroke his hands up and down the backs of her legs. He trailed his lips to one side, nipping at her hip bones and grabbing the lace of her panties with his teeth. He yanked them down and she stepped out of them as he continued to run his hands over her.

"This hardly seems fair," she said as she watched him from above. With a snap of her fingers, his tailored slacks and crisp white shirt disappeared and he was left in nothing but his gloriously smooth skin. The shadowy writing of the tattoo on his left arm drew her attention. How could something so beautiful cause so much pain? He'd said before he would burn the thing from his flesh if he thought it would free him. As much as she loved the way it rippled and moved with his muscle, she would be happy to have it disappear if it saved him from this purgatory.

"I don't know what you're thinking about right now, but let's see if I can make you focus a little, hmmm?" He spoke the words against her flesh and before she could answer, he pulled her into his lap and latched his lips over her breast. She sucked in a breath and exhaled on a moan; all thoughts of the curse gone from her mind. "That's more like it," he said as he shifted his attention to the other breast.

Doria ran her fingers through his hair as she relished the contact with him. Her breaths came short and fast and all she could think about was getting closer to him. She'd share the same skin with this beautiful man if she could. Staying straddled over him, she adjusted herself until she could feel him in just the right place. Then, in an achingly slow movement, she slid her weight down on him fully. Miles moaned in return and it was the most delicious sound she'd ever heard.

Soon, they were moving together in perfect time. The feeling of rightness and joy she had as they fell apart together couldn't have been solely just a dream and she knew then this connection in her mind was as real as anything she could have experienced while awake.

Slumping over his shoulder, she relaxed as she came down from the high. Miles nuzzled into her neck and massaged the muscles of her ass where they met his thighs. "You said you'd found a way to come visit more often," he chucked against her neck.

"Mmm-hmm. I did."

He lifted her gently and lay her down on the sofa. "I like the sound of that."

She nodded and blew out a breath. "More importantly, we've made some progress with the curse."

He sat up quickly at her words. "Tell me."

In a blink, he was dressed again in his soft grey trousers and she was back in her leggings with an oversized t-shirt. "I didn't say you needed to get dressed to tell me." His tone was flat but she recognized it as the teasing he'd intended.

"I wanted us to be able to focus Mr. Oak." She picked up the enormous glass of wine and took another long sip before explaining the information Cassondra had gotten from the university. She ran through the curse as far as she could remember it, and while she felt like she was getting the gist of the words right, she might not have them precisely as the translated copy detailed.

"So, it seems your life here in the bookshop is somehow linked to Peter's. Keeping you trapped here is allowing you both to keep from aging, but he gets the benefit of life out in the world."

He nodded thoughtfully. "I'd guessed at something like this before. He was always into immortality, vampires, and the fountain of youth kind of stuff. I just always thought he was off his rocker."

"But you told me before you offended him or something?" Doria knew Miles had barred Peter Smith from the bookshop at one point, but that alone seemed like a minor slight—certainly not enough to warrant such a terrible revenge.

Miles twisted his lips and ran a hand through his hair. The movement sent the muscles in his chest rippling and Doria had a hard time looking away. He smirked when he saw where her eyes were lingering. "So you get to cover up, but I'm left bare-chested and ripe for the ogling?"

"That sounds about right."

He leaned over and nipped at her ear.

Sighing as he refocused, he went on. "Yes, I kicked him out. I was going through a bit of a tough time in my life." He looked down at his feet, clearly not wanting to meet her eyes.

"Elenor and Cassie told me about your wife," she said gently.

"Sara was more the mother of my son than she was my wife." His eyes held a haunted look when he mentioned Cassie's father. "We were young and I was impulsive. She was kind of a wildcat. After we got married, I thought she'd settle in a little more. I was wrong. William was the world to me, and I could never understand how he couldn't be the world to her too.

"Anyway, she left and I needed an anchor. I was working as an insurance salesman and hated every minute of it. I'd always loved books and I happened by Vespertine one afternoon. Peter had a great window display of adventure stories out and I popped in to check it out. I ended up leaving with a couple and over the next few months I returned several times. Peter said business was bad and he was going to close up shop. The very idea of such a marvelous place shutting its doors forever was beyond my comprehension. I was at the bank the same afternoon and the papers for the sale were done a month later."

It sounded like any normal business transaction to Doria. She furrowed her brow. "But?"

"But even though the deed was in my name and I was the one paying the bills, Peter wanted to act like a managing partner. He showed up every day when I opened and would stay until I closed. He tried to tell me what to stock and how to price things. When I bought the place he had an entire section he kept behind a curtain in the back." Miles jutted his chin in the direction of the furthest shelves. "It was full of all sorts of weird books of the occult. Things you would be surprised even existed at that time. Now you can order all sorts of dark manuals and unsavory tomes. But back then? He had to go to a whole lot of trouble to track those texts down. I told him to take them when the store changed hands. At first, he seemed offended, but then he packed them up with a smirk on his face and carted them out."

Miles plucked the large wineglass from Dorian's hands and took a sip. "Merlot?" he asked and she nodded. He tilted the glass to his lips again before handing it back to her.

"Then it wasn't just what to order, but what I shouldn't keep in stock. Apparently, his dark tastes were fine, but if I had books by certain authors or on certain subjects that he didn't like, he'd insist they should be thrown out. He would occasionally follow people around and snicker at the books they'd choose, making enough people uncomfortable that I had to apologize on the shop's behalf. He'd sneer when I'd bring William along with me for the day, saying the shop wasn't a daycare and why couldn't I get a sitter for him. Better yet, he told me, I should turn him over to the state, seeing as how I was no longer married and didn't have a wife to tend to him."

Doria cringed at the words. She knew it had been a different time and single fathers weren't the thing in the 1950s, but the entire idea of him giving up his child had her stomach twisting in knots. Miles' eyes grew glassy, but he blinked and shook his head as if to clear it. While Doria hoped he'd come to some sort of terms with his son growing up and growing old while he couldn't do the same, she imagined the pain of it would never truly leave him.

"That was the worst of it, but there were other things too. He'd stand too close or make odd little remarks. I'd catch him staring at me with this weird expression on his face. I almost think— well that isn't important." Miles got a slightly embarrassed look on his face and waved a hand as if to brush the thought away.

"What?" Doria prodded.

"Like I said, not important. But looking back on it over many, many, years. . . I think he may have felt we shared some sort of connection and felt rejected when I didn't find an interest in his life or his hobby. At the time it never occurred to me that he could be dangerous. He just was so pesky. One day, I just got tired of it and I told him to leave. He seemed confused like I had no authority to kick him out. But after a few more heated words, I told him I'd call the constable if he didn't get out, or if he showed up again. I realize now I was a little heavy-handed, but he just made my skin crawl. So, yeah. I guess you could say I offended him." He ran his hand through his hair again. "And he got even."

"Miles, I know all about rejection and I can completely relate to being made to feel less than, but this is not even. This is so far beyond even I can't even put it into words. I'm going to kill the ass-wagon if I see him again."

"Ass-wagon?"

"It's a modern term. Or more accurately, a Doria term." She smiled and squeezed his hand.

She bent forward to kiss him again but before her lips connected with his, Doria woke up back in her own bed.

The hot and sticky summer days were filled with more of the same.

Doria working.

Doria trying in vain to find the physical entrance to Vespertine Books.

Doria meeting with Cassie and Elenor to brainstorm anything new that might help them free Miles.

Doria looking forward to the moment her head would hit the pillow and Miles would appear in her dreams.

Doria enjoying all sorts of things while she slept.

Miles seemed over the moon each time she showed up in her nighttime adventures, but she could sense he felt the same as she did. He wanted her in the flesh. A warm physical presence he could hold onto and not lose as soon as her slumber began to lift.

It was for this reason, as well as the need to see him free of the curse, she didn't give up hope.

She was sitting on Elenor's porch one afternoon, face a mere two inches from the rotating floor fan next to her, when the delightfully spunky woman, slapped her arm.

"It's a story!" Elenor barked, eyebrows up to her hairline as if the outburst surprised her just as much as it did Doria.

Doria looked around as if there was a book on the loose, tearing around the porch on wings of its own. "A story?"

Elenor threw her head back and cackled. "A story." She jumped up—in what Doria could only acknowledge was a very spry way for a woman of Elenor's age—and began to do a crazy version of the chicken dance back and forth on the porch.

"I'm still not following. Can you be more specific?" Doria had to fight through her laughter to get the words out.

"The last bit of the curse. Words of merit blah, blah, blah. It has to be a good story. You have to find a truly wonderful story to tell Miles. It will set him free." Elenor grinned.

"Miles is surrounded by really great stories Elenor. I'm sure if it was just a simple novel or whatever, he would have freed himself a long time ago."

The old lady shook her head. "Words of merit born of hate Doria. You said so yourself, you hated all those romance type books. Now you don't. You need to find the right story and read it to him. And it better be a good one."

"That seems kind of easy though doesn't it, Elenor? A little too easy?"

"Doesn't look like anyone's got any better ideas at the moment now does it?" the old lady groused.

"No," Doria admitted. "I don't suppose we do."

For the next two weeks, Doria spent almost all of her free waking hours in the library, searching for the perfect book and nearly every dream moment she shared with Miles doing the same within Vespertine Books.

When she'd asked him if he could think of a tale that might fit the bill, he shrugged and raised his hands. "It could be any one of hundreds of thousands of stories."

Doria had the same feeling, but she was disappointed just the same. Some small part of her wanted to think Miles would magically come up with the perfect book, just as he had many times before. He'd been able to feel her passion for reading and steer her in the right direction so many times before, why couldn't he do it just this once more?

She was standing in her favorite section of the store, the end cap between the horror novels and the romantic suspense books. She'd found a random romantic fantasy stuffed on the shelf. The lovely book was a bright raspberry pink with beautiful silver foil lettering on the cover. The edges were sprayed in a matching pattern with silver and grey swirls of magic over a soft pink edge. It was definitely out of place. Doria tucked it in the crook of her arm and made her way to the correct shelf.

"Miles?" She asked to pull his attention away from a rack of new releases. "How do you get the new books?"

"No idea." He said plainly. "They just show up?"

"Well, what do you do with the money people spend on them?"

One side of his mouth quirked up. "No one spends money in here Doria. People will occasionally wander in and browse—I used to love it when that happened—but no one ever actually tried to purchase anything. As soon as they seem interested, something calls them away and they leave empty-handed. The shop keeps tabs I guess. Old books go away and new ones appear. Only Cassie, Elenor, and William ever took books out, but they always brought them back. You were the first person outside my family to leave with one of my books."

She didn't know why but knowing that made Doria even sadder than she had been.

She decided to change the subject. "Summer's coming to an end soon. Isn't your one night of freedom sometime in the autumn?"

"It is."

"Good. I fully hope to have found the right book before then, but if not, I am going to hunt you down that night and spend every moment of it with you."

He pulled his glasses off and blinked at her. "Yes. I don't know why I didn't think of that myself."

She walked over to kiss him just as the bookshop began to shimmer and shift.

When Doria awoke in her bed, she was clutching a gorgeous pink and grey bound book. Apparently, it hadn't gotten reshelved after all.

7

FELICITY had been in the shower for hours and Doria was getting tired of waiting. Pulling the book from her dream was utter insanity and she needed to unpack how she felt about it with someone. She'd already paced around the tiny living room for an insanely long period of time and if she didn't talk to her roommate soon, she was sure to lose her mind.

Banging on the door in warning, Doria pushed into the cramped bathroom and yanked back the shower curtain.

Felicity yelped, but not as loudly as the tall well-built man who currently had her up against the shower wall. He spun around and yanked the curtain from Doria's grasp in a failed attempt to cover himself as Felicity broke into hysterical giggles.

"Jeez, Peaches. If you wanted to join in, you could have just asked."

Doria's face flushed as her mouth dropped open. "I am so. . . so. . . sorry," she stammered. "I'll just leave you two to it."

She turned on her heel and dashed from the bathroom.

Not wanting to have any awkward encounters, she grabbed the book she'd somehow brought out of the dream and locked herself behind her bedroom door.

Having nothing else to do, she cracked open the spine and began to read.

Banking on Fortune

Rose Benston tucked an errant chestnut curl behind her ear as she counted out a stack of crisp five-dollar bills. The clacking of typewriter keys mingled with the murmurs of customer voices in the grand marble hall of the First National Bank of New York. Rose handed the money to Mrs. Clements, an elderly woman with a black beaded cloche perched snuggly atop her gray head. Mrs. Clements was a Thursday regular. Always at the bank at precisely the same time, to make the same withdrawal, every Thursday, rain or shine.

Rose wondered what she did with the money. Perhaps she lunched with the ladies each day or perhaps she played the ponies. Or perhaps she did nothing at all, but keep the cash squirreled away in a cookie jar at her expensive downtown apartment. Who was to say?

"Thank you, my dear," Mrs. Clements said. "You're always so quick with my service."

Rose flashed a dimpled smile. "My pleasure, Mrs. Clements. You have a lovely rest of your day."

As the older lady toddled away, Rose neatened the stack of papers on her counter, then turned to help the next customer in line. She loved the fast pace of the bank. It made the day melt away almost as soon as it began. She also enjoyed the sense of purpose it gave her and allowed her to lead the independent life she so loved. Someday, she hoped to rise from her perch at the teller window to one of the offices upstairs. She could practically picture her name etched in the frosted glass and smell the polish on the hardwood desk.

"Good morning, Mr. Jenks," Rose said brightly as a rather portly man stepped up to her window. More silver dollars today?"

The man chuckled as he mopped his damp brow with a handkerchief. "You know me too well Miss Benston. I'll take two rolls if you please."

Rose nodded and quickly retrieved the coins. As she counted them out, she overheard two other tellers whispering about a group of important visitors coming to visit the following week. Her pulse quickened, but she maintained her composure. It would take more than a few bits of rumor to distract her from her job.

Mr. Jenks tipped his cap goodbye and Rose took a deep breath as the next customer approached—an elderly gentleman with a stern face and piercing hawkish eyes.

"Good morning, sir," Rose said. "How can I help you today?"

The man peered down his nose at her. "There seems to be a problem with my account," he said crisply. "I made a sizeable deposit yesterday and it does not appear to have been processed."

Rose maintained a polite smile despite the accusation in the man's tone. "I'm very sorry to hear that. May I take a look at your records?"

The man slid a bank book across the counter. Rose reviewed the ledger, her brow furrowing. There was no indication of the transaction at all.

"You're absolutely correct, nothing was recorded," Rose said. "Please accept my apologies. We may have made an error."

The man's glare intensified. "This is unacceptable."

Rose hesitated. She wasn't authorized to correct an error of this magnitude. "If you'll just give me a moment, I'll be happy to confer with my manager. We'll get this all sorted."

Within a handful of minutes, the manager had things straightened out and the man left on his way.

"That man can be a real bear, I tell you," a familiar voice said at her side.

Rose turned to see her dear friend Gertrude sliding onto the stool beside her. Gert's auburn waves bounced as she checked herself in the reflection of her desk lamp.

"You don't know the half of it, Gert," Rose said, rolling her eyes. "He was fit to be tied."

"Say, why don't we go to Klein's today for lunch?" Gert suggested. "My treat even."

"That sounds divine." Rose was nearly salivating thinking of the warm bread and thick-cut roast beef the little diner was known for. She glanced at the ornate clock above the bank entrance. "I'm due for my break in twenty minutes."

After locking down her window, Rose joined Gert as she gathered her belongings, and the pair headed out into the bustling New York streets. Vendors called out their wares, shoeshines beckoned, and brightly painted taxis honked impatiently amidst the snarled traffic. Rose loved the cacophony and happily linked her arm through Gertrude's as they navigated the heavily populated sidewalks.

Soon they arrived at the dingy little diner. Gert ordered creamed chicken on toast while Rose opted for her go-to sandwich.

"Wouldn't it be grand to have one of the charming little flats up there?" Gertrude mused, tipping her head to indicate the towering building across the street. "Looking down on all the poor saps who have to hoof it from home to work here and back again?"

"I dream of it every day." Rose agreed evenly. "The way I'd decorate. Who I'd invite over for parties. The music I'd play when I opened the windows to let the breeze blow through."

Gert set down her teacup and leaned forward eagerly. "Just think, Rose. Someday, we could start up a little business. Maybe it'd grow enough to land us in one of those flats."

Rose scoffed. "If you've got an idea, I'm all ears."

Gertrude reclined in her chair, the same far-off dreamy look she always got when discussing the topic. "A girl can dream, can't she."

"Yes." Rose nodded. "Yes, she can."

The following day, James Montgomery strode into the bank, his expensive leather loafers tapping against the marble floor. He was always put together. Hair combed back and neatly trimmed. Briefcase polished to a high shine. Pocket watch and pocket square always perfectly placed. The suit on his back was worth more than Rose made in a month.

Straightening up the papers on her counter, Rose avoided his gaze. Her boss's presence always made the hairs on the back of her neck stand on end. He was young for a bank executive—probably no more than forty— and handsome enough, but everything about him screamed at Rose to keep her distance.

"Rose, in my office. Now." His tone left little room for argument.

Her stomach twisted in knots as she followed him.

What had she done wrong this time? Miscounted a deposit? Said something unprofessional to one of her colleagues? Nothing came to mind.

She nervously sat in the firm high-backed chair across from his desk. Mr. Montgomery settled into his own chair and steepled his fingers studying her. His eyes were cold and gray. They brought to mind snow clouds on a subfreezing day.

"I have an assignment for you," he said tersely from the other side of his massive oak desk.

Rose clasped her hands together in her lap, forcing herself not to fidget. "Of course, sir."

"Several of our most. . . influential clients will be in the city next week. I'm putting you in charge of seeing to their needs." A predatory smile crept across his face. "I'll make sure you have the funds to entertain them properly. Do whatever is necessary to keep them happy. Do you understand?"

Rose's cheeks flushed as his meaning became clear. "I'm not sure I'm the right person for this particular assignment sir."

"Sure you are. You're young and quite attractive. I'm sure you know all the best places to take them out. Gather some of your friends and keep them company. You know wine and dine them?"

"I'm not—"

He cut her off. "It'll only be for an evening. If you do a good job, perhaps we can work out some sort of promotion to a better position for you."

Rose bit at her lower lip even as bile rose in her throat. It was only one night. She could convince Gert and a few of the other tellers to tag along. They could all laugh about it later in the break room.

She nodded stiffly and Mr. Montgomery chuckled. "You're a quick learner Rose. I like that."

The following day, Rose was once again summoned to James Montgomery's office. This time, he had two of the other partners with him, Mr. Thompson and Mr. Finkle. Rose stood by the door, trying to appear unobtrusive, but every other minute, she caught Mr. Montgomery's eyes traveling to her.

As they finished discussions of a merger, her boss explained to the other men, "I've put Rose here in charge of the entertainment for next week's visit." He tapped out his cigarette on the edge of a beautiful cobalt ashtray.

Rose ran her hands down the length of her slim pencil skirt and forced a tight smile as the partners turned to look at her.

Thompson, a balding man with a rather large bulbous nose grinned lasciviously. "Perhaps I'll invite myself to the festivities. What is you've got planned?"

"I'm not sure yet sir," Rose's grin grew tighter. "There's a new cocktail lounge down on the corner. Perhaps just music and drinks."

"Sounds divine." He turned away in dismissal.

"Is there anything else you'll be needing from me Mr. Montgomery?" she asked edging her way toward the door.

"Not at the moment, but pop in here before you clock out for the night."

Rose nodded and returned to her window, sweat beading along her collar and dampening her palms.

She finished with her regular duties and closed out her window, then with a stomach full of dread, made her way to James Montgomery's office as she'd been instructed.

She found her boss leaning against the window frame, staring out into the crowded city a few stories below. A glass of bourbon dangled from one hand.

"Close the door, Rose." He didn't turn from the view as he addressed her, but she did as he asked. "You've always been a diligent employee. It's one of the many things I admire about you. Consistently doing what is required."

He turned and stared at the reports scattered on his desk. "These can wait until tomorrow, I think. What do you say to joining me for dinner instead?"

Rose's mouth went dry. This was new. He'd never been direct in his interest before. Always a sideling look standing a bit too close. Things she could easily ignore or explain away. She searched for an excuse, some way to refuse him without provoking an angry reaction.

"I'm sorry, Mr. Montgomery," she said. "I have plans for the evening."

"Well then, cancel them. I'm sure whatever it is can't be all that important." He stepped around the desk and Rose instinctively retreated toward the door.

He frowned and tipped his head, eyes studying her. "I would really appreciate it if you would accompany me to dinner this evening Rose." He'd stepped closer and tucked her hair behind her ear then wrapped his fingers around the back of her neck.

Rose stiffened and grabbed his hand to dislodge it from her body. "I apologize for any misunderstanding Mr. Montgomery," she said. "I'm not interested in a romantic relationship."

His eyes narrowed further. "I don't for one moment believe that to be true. I've seen the way you look at me."

All she could think was how she never looked at him. She avoided his gaze at every opportunity. James Montgomery had to know that. But he always got what he wanted and now it seemed he wanted her.

He crowded her even further, placing his hands on either side of her head where it rested against the closed door to his office. "Come now Ms. Benston," he said softly. Rose winced against the thick smell of alcohol washing over her. "Don't pretend you don't want this. Everyone wants this." He removed one of his hands and swept it around the office. "Power, wealth, status. A step up from that teller window. A step out of the seedier side of the city. All you have to do is agree to have dinner with me."

Revulsion tore at her. She placed her hands on his chest and shoved. Hard. He stumbled back, shock on his face. He recovered quickly however and shock turned to a flash of anger.

"I want nothing from you, least of all your affections." She straightened her blouse where it tucked into her skirt. *"Now if you'll excuse me, I'd like to head home for the evening."*

The rage was gone from his face, now replaced by an oily smile. *"My apologies,"* he said. *"I seem to have misunderstood the situation. Have a pleasant evening, Rose."*

He returned to his desk and threw down the remaining bourbon in his glass before turning his attention to the reports before him. Rose exited as quickly as she could, remembering to clock out just before she fled to the comfort of her tiny apartment in the seedier part of the city.

The following day, a small bunch of flowers greeted her when she approached her window. A small card attached read, *"My apologies for last evening. Please allow me to make amends."*

Rose deposited the card in the waste receptacle and left the flowers in the break room for all of the girls to enjoy.

Each day for a week, a similar bunch greeted her. Save for the first bouquet, none had a note attached, but she knew who had left them just the same.

On the sixth day—the night Rose and her friends were responsible for entertaining the bank investors—instead of an assortment of daisies and carnations, a single pale pink rose was left.

"Holy moly Rose," Gertrude said when she saw it. *"I don't know who's got it bad for you, but I guess you're making him work for it, huh?"*

Rose grimaced and placed a hand on the back of her neck. *"It isn't like that. I don't want. . .It isn't. . . I'm not interested."*

"I can see that," Gert said as Rose left to take the flower to the break room. Maybe one of the other ladies would enjoy it. *"But hey, I got you a little something to put them in any way."*

Rose turned to see Gert digging in her bag. She came up with a lovely, albeit slightly tarnished, pewter vessel.

"I don't think it's real silver or anything, but I got it for a steal at the little junk shop on the corner by my place. It was in the window yesterday and just thought it might hold all those fancy flowers you've been getting."

"Ah, Gert. You didn't need to do that."

"I know, but we need to start decorating that future pad of ours sometime."

"Well, I can't just leave it here. I'll take this one home," she nodded at the rose, "tonight, and keep the vase there."

She made it through the day without any hiccups. Late in the afternoon, a group of four older men made their way through the lobby and to the elevator. Rose cringed and looked helplessly at Gertrude. Gert finished up with her customer and smiled back. "It's only one night. We'll get through it."

As they clocked out, Rose grabbed the metal vase and the pink Rose it held. It wasn't ideal to take it with her on the night's outing, but she didn't want to leave it over the weekend.

James Montgomery and Mr. Thompson appeared with the visiting investors. Rose smiled through the introductions and explained they would be walking the short distance to the cocktail lounge for drinks. Gertrude and two other tellers, both young unattached women, had agreed to tag along in moral support. It wasn't until the group had left the building that Rose realized James Montgomery was tagging along as well.

Her face must have shown her unease. "Something the matter Miss Benston?" Mr. Montgomery asked.

"Not at all, sir. I just didn't realize you were planning to join us this evening," Rose replied.

"Can't let these fellows have all the fun now, can I?" He smiled good-naturedly at the men surrounding him. His comment was met with smiles and a few chuckles; even a slap on the shoulder.

Rose plastered on a smile and stepped closer to Gert.

The cocktail lounge was crowded even at such an early hour. Faint jazz drifted through the smoke-filled air. The party took up two tables in the back corner and despite the terrible company, Rose had to admit, she liked the atmosphere almost as much as the martini she ordered.

Thankfully, the evening went off without a hitch. The investors were relatively well behaved and the woman enjoyed the music and drinks. Even James Montgomery seemed to relax a touch. Rose was beginning to feel like she was going to make it out of the night unscathed and could feel herself relax just a bit.

"Well gentleman," she said a couple of hours later. "It's time for me and Gertrude to head home. I do hope you've enjoyed the evening. There will be cab service outside to get you all safely home."

Gert and the other women said their goodbyes and the four of them stood to leave.

"Just a moment, Miss Benston." Mr. Montgomery stood and cut her off as she was leaving.

Rose's heart sank.

"You forgot something," he said as she turned. In his hand, he held the metal vase and the single flower he'd left her earlier in the day. She'd set it on the table and in her urge to leave, had almost left it behind.

"Thank you." She accepted the flower and headed for the door before he could waylay her further.

A light knocking sounded at Doria's bedroom door. Pulling herself from the story, she tucked a receipt from the cosmetics store in the pages to hold her place. She really needed to find an actual bookmark.

"Come on in Fel," she said as a return flood of embarrassment crashed through her.

Her roommate sauntered in with a mug of coffee in one hand and a sprinkled donut in the other. She took a sip of the coffee before setting it on Doria's dresser and plopping down on the foot of her bed.

"So. I assume there must be something urgent for you to pull that little stunt." There was a wicked gleam in her eye as she spoke.

Doria dropped her head in her hand and rolled over on her side, not wanting to make eye contact with her roommate. "I'm so sorry." The pillow her face was buried in muffled the words.

Felicity laughed her off. "Don't be. I think Mik was secretly a little turned on by the whole thing. Well. . . he was after he got over the initial shock."

"Mik, huh? He's the flavor of the week? What happened to Landon?"

"Landon was too much of a pretty boy. But Mik? All *man*. Oh, I *really* like him, Doria. I'm going to see if I can't get this one to stick around awhile."

Doria wouldn't say she was shocked exactly. But she was certainly surprised. For as long as they'd been friends, Felicity has enjoyed playing the field. To hear she might want to make something long-term was kind of nice.

"If you want him to stick around, he will most assuredly stick around."

"You think so?"

"Absolutely."

"Thanks, Peaches. So, what was so important?" Felicity took a bite of her donut and Doria watched as sprinkles fell into her lap. Felicity picked them up one by one and nibbled them off her fingers.

Doria proceeded to tell Felicity about waking up with the pink and silver book in her bed and how she was sure it must be some sort of a sign. "It has to be this story right? Otherwise, why would it show up here?"

"I don't know, but you better get back to reading. Maybe if you're lucky you can read it to Miles tonight and by tomorrow this whole thing will be over with."

"Damn, but I hope you're right."

Felicity kissed her on the cheek and took her donut and coffee out to the living room. Doria heard deep male laughter and assumed Mik must still be there.

She looked down at the book. While it was set in New York, rather than a small town, it took place in the mid-twentieth century and the era had her thinking of Miles. It was one more tiny detail that seemed to reinforce the notion that this was *THE BOOK*, to help break his curse. She couldn't for the life of her however figure how it would turn into either a fantasy or a romance. The only man in the story was a complete douche and even going for an enemies to lovers vibe was going to be a stretch. Only one way to find out. She continued to read.

A block down, Rose and Gert caught the bus. It gave Rose a sense of relief to be seated next to her friend.

The heavy vase grew warm in her hands. She held it up to study it more closely and squinted in the dim light trying to make out the intricately carved decorations crawling from the base to the lip. It was about ten inches high with a wide base and narrow neck. Slim filagree handles ran from opposite sides near the lip and swirled down to connect roughly halfway to the bottom.

"I'm not sure this is actually a vase, Gert," Rose said as she peered at the object in her hand.

Gertrude shrugged. "Maybe not. Just dump the water out when you get home." She stood and squeezed Rose's shoulder. "This is me. I'll see ya on Monday."

"You bet." Rose hardly looked up from the warming metal. Gert was almost off the bus when she realized she was being rude. Lifting her head she called, "Thanks again, Gert."

Two stops later, Rose exited the bus and headed for home. As she walked the metal grew warmer and warmer where it rested in her palm. She paused under a streetlamp and examined the vase more closely. In the light, the intricate etchings were even more stunning. Her fingers traced the swirls and flourished engraved into the metal.

"What are you?" she murmured.

The metal, tarnished though it was, seemed to twinkle in the lamplight. She shook her head, laughing softly to herself. "I must be losing it, talking to a hunk of old junk," she said wryly.

Her apartment was dark and quiet when she unlocked the door. Kicking off her kitten heels; she made a beeline for the small kitchen. Rummaging in the fridge, she made herself a cold plate of chicken. The pale pink rose was relegated to an old mayonnaise jar after she fetched her silver polish and a relatively clean rag from under the sink.

Cradling the metal in both hands, she studied it again before placing it on the table. She ate her chicken, never taking her eyes off the beautiful container. When she was done, she pushed the plate to the side and grabbed the small tin of polish. She ran a thin coat around the entirety of the vessel then set to work scrubbing it until it gleamed. With every swipe of the rag, the metal began to shimmer and shine—not like any silver or pewter she'd seen before. In a matter of moments, the thing practically glowed in her hands. And it was warmer still. Almost hot to the touch.

Nervous, she placed the gleaming thing back on the table. As she did so, wisps of faint lilac smoke began pouring from the narrow opening at the top. As the cloud thickened, it darkened to an intense periwinkle. The aroma of cinnamon and some other spice she couldn't name filled the air.

Rose pushed herself back from the table, ready to grab a glass of water should the thing combust. But rather than flames pouring from the top, the smoke swirled and solidified into a towering figure with brilliant aquamarine eyes and dark copper hair immaculately cut tight at the sides and slightly longer on top.

Rose stood so abruptly her chair knocked over behind her. She backed up to the far side of the kitchen—which wasn't far at all—heart thundering in her chest.

Ah. The fantasy, at last.

The smoke continued to pour from the vase and swirl around the figure's waist and thighs. Then, like a candle being extinguished by a breath, the smoke billowed briefly then retracted but continued to hang in the air. The figure stepped forward, out of the vase, and down onto the linoleum. The smoke evaporated as if it had never been there.

The man rolled his impressive shoulders and neck, closed his eyes in a sign of pure relief, and sighed. It was only after opening them that he seemed to take note of Rose cowering on the other side of the room. He crossed his arms and looked at her with a bored expression.

"No need to cower."

She didn't know how to respond to such a ridiculous statement.

"What. . . Who are you?" she finally managed to ask.

"I thought it was obvious. I'm the djinn you have summoned."

"But I haven't summoned a—"

"A djinn. And you obviously did. You're there and I am here. Unless there is someone else lurking about?" he replied.

"No. There's no one else here." There was no one else there. *Rose was alone in her apartment with this thing and no one would think to look for her until Monday.*

She began to tremble even more violently.

The djinn cocked a single elegant eyebrow in her direction. "I'm not going to harm you. You summoned me." As if that should all be perfectly clear.

"But I didn't. I was just polishing the vase," she looked at the gleaming metal container where it rested behind the enormous hulking man taking up way too much space in her tiny kitchen.

"It isn't a vase." He explained. "It is my prison." He glanced behind him and sneered at the hunk of metal polished to a high shine. "It hasn't been that clean in ages."

He turned back to her. "By rubbing the infernal thing, you have summoned me and freed me from my confinement. I am duty bound to serve you."

"Serve me?" she squeaked. "Serve me how?"

"That is not up to me to decide." The djinn wasn't the tallest man Rose had ever seen, but he was imposing nonetheless. He wore a simple white shirt open at the collar and dark grey trousers.

"I don't understand."

"It's not for me to decide," he said again. "You may request three things from me. I will fulfill those requests to the best of my ability. There is a certain amount of magic involved and once the task is completed it can't be undone."

"And it can be anything?"

He tilted his head to the side. "No. Not anything. I can't make you immortal. I can't make you a djinn. I can't bring a loved one back from the dead. I can't grant you unlimited wishes. Some wish for fame. Others for fortune. Still others wish for love."

Rose's breath caught. She expected him to say more. That list was fairly limited. Her head was spinning. It couldn't be real.

"I'll need some time to think about it," she finally said.

Again, his elegant eyebrow quirked up. "As you wish. I'll be waiting for your decision."

To her surprise, the djinn smiled and sauntered into her living room where he dropped down on the couch.

"What are you doing?" Her voice rose in pitch with each word.

"I'm waiting."

"I didn't mean I was going to make a wish tonight."

"I didn't think you had."

"So, you're just going to stay here until I do?" She couldn't have that. People would begin to talk. It was bad enough she was a woman alone in the city. Working at a bank no less. While a decade earlier women had done all manner of jobs to get America through the second great war, most young women were married and raising children now. Her landlady would throw her out on the street if she thought a handsome young man was living with her.

Handsome. Was he handsome, she asked herself.

Yes. Yes, he was.

"Well, I'm not going back into those tight quarters. Not until you've gotten your requests and my service to you is no longer bound." He crossed one foot over his knee and smiled at her. *"I can assure you, your virtue is safe. I'm perfectly capable of keeping myself hidden and keeping my hands to myself."*

She hadn't even considered him not *keeping his hands to himself.* Death and dismemberment yes, but not. . . Her face flushed brightly as she paced in front of him.

"I'll just request your payment then. I can have anything other than the items you listed before?" If she could get him to grant her three wishes, he would be on his way and she could rest easily.

"Yes," he said slowly, *"but I warn you, magic can be very tricky, so you're going to want to think about what you request. And I can only grant one thing in any given cycle of the sun, so it'll do you no good to rattle off three things right here and now."*

"So, I'm stuck with you for three days, regardless?" She felt herself deflate.

"I will be with you until the contract is complete, yes."

Rose thought about her options. It was still best to get the first request over with so she could see this through *sooner rather than later. But what did she want? Not fame. Being in the spotlight was never her dream. She did want to fall in love one day, but she'd prefer it if it wasn't due to some magical spell. Fortune? She had no wish to be overly wealthy, but then her mind drifted back to her earlier conversation with Gertrude and their desire to live in a fancy uptown loft.*

"I'd like to be in a position where I can live comfortably and not worry over my finances." She stood before him, wringing her fingers together.

When she looked at him, she thought disappointment flashed briefly across his face. "You're sure, this is your desire? It can't be stopped once I set things into motion."

She played it around in her head. He said magic could be tricky, but this seemed safe enough.

"Yes," she paused. "I don't even know your name."

"That is correct." He reclined further onto the couch cushions.

"Well," she said exasperated. "What is it?"

"Not something you shall learn this night."

She huffed. "I'm Rose. But I don't suppose you care about that do you?"

"Not particularly. Now Rose, are you sure you desire this service from me?" the djinn asked.

She nodded.

"I need to hear it."

"Yes. I'd like for you to put me in a position of financial security." She took a breath and tacked on, "So I can afford to live in one of the lovely uptown lofts."

Rose leaned back from him, squinting one eye and a grimace tightening her cheeks, unsure if he'd be angry about the addendum.

He sighed, crossed his arms over his chest, and nodded.

8

ROSE straightened her emerald taffeta gown and took a steadying breath. These events always made her uncomfortable. Across the ballroom, James strode through the crowd, his handsome features creased into a cunning smile. Rose knew that look, and no matter how she tried to tell herself otherwise, it always made her cringe inside.

"Rose my darling, you look simply ravishing." James bowed and kissed her hand. His lips lingered and it sent a shiver up her spine.

Wait. What?

Doria flipped to the previous page and looked at the number. Were pages missing from the book? No. The page numbers were in order. It seemed like a weird transition and not one she'd seen coming, but the only way to figure it out was to keep reading.

"Rose my darling, you look simply ravishing." James bowed and kissed her hand. His lips lingered and it sent a shiver up her spine.

She blushed, glancing around to ensure no one had noticed.

"Relax. Let the world see," he said. "I want them all to know you're mine."

Her cheeks burned. She hated every bit of this.

James slid an arm possessively around her waist. "Sooner or later, you'll need to admit you feel the same."

Something tickled at the back of her mind. She just couldn't remember when she'd gone from loathing James Montgomery to tolerating him, and finally to welcoming his advances.

Now she was dating James and had even agreed to move into the loft he had just a few blocks from the bank. Although he maintained his own residence further uptown, he often popped in to see her there. She no longer worked at the teller window but rather had been made his personal assistant. She heard the whispers and gossip fluttering around downstairs every day. The other women no longer invited her to sit with them at lunch and even Gertrude seemed to be shunning her.

"I can't James. These people just see me as some loose gold digger."

"Then marry me."

She stared at him. "What?"

His smile widened and became even more predatory. "Marry me, Rose. Let's announce our engagement right now. In front of everyone."

Her heart pounded. She didn't want to marry James. She knew it in her gut, but she couldn't explain why she'd let herself get dragged into this situation in the first place.

"I'm tired of waiting." His eyes glinted with a malicious triumph. "Marry me, Rose."

Her head was swimming. She couldn't imagine saying yes, but how could she explain it to James? He'd given her everything she'd ever wanted. Stability, security.

Her eyes darted through the ballroom looking for any excuse. A waiter on the far side of the space caught her glance. He moved fluidly between guests, handing out champagne in delicate fluted glasses. The tray swayed and dipped as he meandered through the crowd, but not a drop was spilled. Turning in her direction, Rose felt an immediate connection with the man. He had startling eyes, a bright aquamarine. With one of those eyes, he tipped her a wink before turning his back on her again.

Rose's breath caught in her throat. She knew him.

In a flash, her memory of earlier in the evening slammed into her head. The djinn. I warn you, magic can be very tricky. *Tricky indeed. How dare he do this to her? His idea of security was being tied to a man she not only didn't love but that she loathed?*

This was his doing. Somehow this was all due to her wish. She hadn't been dating James Montgomery for months or even weeks. She hadn't been dating him at all. Not until she'd foolishly asked the djinn to grant her the security and resources to live in a posh uptown loft.

James sensing her shift in attention, glanced over his shoulder to see who she was looking at. He frowned deeply. When Rose looked back at the waiter, the djinn was gone.

Without so much as a warning, James raised his voice and clinked the side of his glass. "Can I get everyone's attention please?"

Rose felt her stomach plummet. What was he doing?

James continued. "I'd like to make a toast. Well, more of an announcement really, but a toast as well." James turned to her and the wolf was back in his smile. "Some of you may not be aware, but I'd like everyone to know Miss Rose Benston is the center of my world." It was shocking how easily the lie fell from his lips. Money was the center of James' world Rose knew. "And this evening, she has agreed to become my wife."

No. No. No. This couldn't be happening. She'd never agreed. She hadn't said anything actually.

"*Please. Let's all raise our glasses to the future Mrs. James Montgomery.*"

The room erupted into cheers and applause. Rose accepted a glass of champagne with numb fingers. She couldn't bring herself to raise it to her lips. The bubbles seemed to mock her, reminiscent of the life and joy and freedom that were slipping so easily through her fingers.

When the applause died down, Rose looked at James. "If you'll excuse me, I'm not feeling well."

"What has gotten into you tonight Rose?"

"I. . . I. . .I think I'll just head home if it's all the same to you."

"Of course, it's not all the same to me. Tonight is important. You know that." He stepped closer, a sneer marring his perfect features.

Rose backed up a step as her hand fluttered to her neckline. "Of course. I'm sorry. It's just this talk of engagements that has me feeling flustered. Maybe I'll just go sit for a moment?" She looked up at him for permission. His features smoothed back into the composed handsome man he liked projecting to the world.

"Don't go far." He ran his fingers along her jaw and placed a quick peck on her temple. "I'll find you before the speeches begin."

Rose made her way to the entrance of the ballroom, her pulse pounding and her stomach close to revolt. She had to find the djinn and make him fix this.

The thick taffeta of her gown rustled as she pushed through the door and nearly ran straight into the creature in question. Dressed now in a crisp tuxedo, he made quite the picture.

Before she could open her mouth to unleash who knew what on him, he raised a hand and shook his head. "Now, before you go completely mad, I did try to warn you."

"You did no such thing!"

"Didn't I? I do remember telling you to be very careful with how you wished for me to serve you." His tone was mild but Rose could swear there was laughter in his eyes.

"But why would you do this? Why James Montgomery? I never said I wanted to get married and certainly not to him." She pitched her voice low, not wanting to be overheard.

"Why not him? He's handsome and powerful and he is more than able to provide you with the financial resources you so desired." The djinn raised his eyebrows and smirked.

"And he's vile." Rose's voice cracked on the words as she struggled not to cry.

The smirk quickly fell as the djinn's eyebrows lowered into a frown. "How do you mean?"

"He's not. . ." she dropped her head and shook it. "Never mind. It doesn't matter. I'll just use my second wish to put this back the way it was."

"You can't. Not yet. I told you only one wish per day and while it seems as though more time has passed, it hasn't. You must wait until tomorrow." He tipped his chin to look at her more closely. "He hasn't hurt you before, has he? Done something he shouldn't?"

Rose blew out a long breath. "Nothing more than an unwanted touch or two." She looked around. "I know I'm supposed to stay here, be supportive and all that, but I don't think I can manage it."

"Then let's get you home." The djinn extended his elbow and despite herself, Rose took it willingly. When they made it to the street, she turned to head toward the bus stop, but the djinn made a 'tsking' sound and pointed to the upscale building on the corner.

"You live there now."

Rose's eyes traveled up in the direction of his extended finger. She had to crane her head back to get a glimpse of the windows. At least that part of the wish had worked. He escorted her through the revolving glass to where a doorman waited.

"Hello, Miss Benston. Early evening for you?" The doorman asked.

The doorman obviously knew her, and with a slight shift of her focus, she realized she knew him too. Walter. His name was Walter. The magic that had gotten her into this position left no holes.

Suddenly Rose was worried about the djinn at her side. What would the doorman think of her bringing a waiter home with her?

"Hello Walter, this is. . ." she turned to where the djinn had been just behind her. The space was empty. "Sorry. Yes. An early evening for me. Have a good night."

The doorman pushed a button on the elevator and dipped his head. "If you need anything, don't hesitate to ring down Miss Benston."

The elevator doors slid shut with a ding and Rose nearly jumped out of her skin as the djinn appeared. He leaned casually against the wall. "Jumpy, jumpy."

"How did you. . .?" She shook her head. "Never mind." She closed her eyes and leaned back as the car climbed higher into the building. Suddenly her eyes flew open. "Wait a minute. If you can just disappear like that, there was never really any need for me to make my first wish tonight. You could have just stayed hidden for the landlady."

"That is correct." He grinned at her. "You pick up quickly."

"Well then, why didn't you say so?"

"I did. Sort of. You didn't ask me to elaborate."

"And if I had?"

He ticked his head back and forth, lips turned down in contemplation. "I suppose that depends on how nicely you phrased the question."

The elevator dinged and the door opened on a hall carpeted in a deep plush. The walls were creamy smooth and dotted with bits of modern art. It was the nicest place Rose had ever seen.

"I live here?" Her eyes widened. "I live here." She smiled but it was fleeting. "I live here for tonight. Tomorrow, we are fixing this whole thing."

"Your wish will be my command." The bored expression had returned to the djinn's handsome face. The cheekbones alone were enough to have Rose blushing slightly.

Without needing to ask, she turned and walked halfway down the hall before stopping and retrieving a key from her clutch. Letting them into the spacious apartment, she sighed. Knowing she hadn't lived here at all didn't make her mind rid itself of the memories of the past several months spent in the luxurious space. It was starting to drive her crazy. Knowing none of it was true, but feeling like it was. The space was easily three times her own small apartment. Tomorrow, she'd return to her previous home and make sure the djinn erased all traces of this place from her. That didn't mean she couldn't enjoy it for the night.

"I'm going to take a bath." She dropped her things on the entryway table and slipped out of the heels she'd donned for the evening.

As she crossed into her bedroom, the sight of the gleaming metallic vase brought her up short. She still didn't know the djinn's name and for some reason, the thought bothered her. Calling over her shoulder, she let him know as much. "I really would feel better knowing your name if you're to spend the night on my sofa."

"Who said anything about the sofa."

Rose squealed as the djinn's voice came from directly in front of her where he was resting comfortably on her bed. He'd traded in his waiter's tuxedo for his loose-fitting grey trousers. Only the grey trousers. No shirt, no shoes, and apparently, no modesty. His muscular arms were stretched back and his head rested in his hands. His long legs were stretched out before him and crossed at the ankle.

"You can't be in here. I'm getting ready to bathe." Rose was scandalized. "And in case you don't remember, you've just gotten me engaged to another man."

He waved a hand through the air. "We'll sort that all. To be fair, at the time I had no idea you didn't want the handsome, successful, wealthy guy. It's what most women wish for."

"I am not most women." She gave him her most scathing look and he smiled. "And I still want to know your name."

"Maybe you should wish for it." He winked at her. Whatever he saw in her face had him close to laughing. "I promise not to look. Besides this is what? 1953? Not like its Puritan England." He yawned. "That was a brutal time, let me tell you."

"How old are you?" Rose asked.

"Old enough to not care anymore."

"And how often are you out of the vessel?" She was genuinely curious.

"Why do you ask? Planning to send me back soon enough, aren't you?" His eyes remained closed but Rose could have sworn there was a touch of bitterness in his voice.

"Well, no. I don't care if you go back. You can stay here for the rest of your life if you like."

He opened one eye and looked at her.

"Well not here, obviously. I'm not even staying here." She gestured around the room, hands flapping slightly. "But out in the world. Not in the vase or the prison or whatever it is."

His voice was quiet when he spoke. "That, I am afraid, is not entirely up to you."

"Who is it up to?" She asked just as quietly.

"The magic. The universe. The order of time and all it entails," his words were flippant, but the meaning was clear. When her brow furrowed, he continued. "It's what I am. What I was created for. To serve the magic. I'm allowed out when I am summoned and as soon as my job is complete, I return to my cage to await another summons. It's been this way since the beginning, and unless certain steps are taken, it will be this way until the end."

"What steps?"

He pursed his lips. "I am not at liberty to say."

"That doesn't seem fair."

"Sorry to disappoint you."

"No. Not that you can't tell me, but that you're trapped in there."

He sighed. "I appreciate your concern. Some things are just out of our control. Now go and take your bath."

Rose was awoken several hours later to a loud banging on her door.

"Rose. Open this door immediately." James' voice was loud and rather angry. "Open this door Rose, or so help me I will wake everyone in this building and tell them what sort of person you truly are."

Scurrying up, Rose looked over to see the djinn fast asleep. In her bed. He most definitely had not been there when she'd dozed off.

Pulling on her dressing gown, she hissed at him. "Wake up."

He groaned and rolled over. Still shirtless, and now sleep tousled, Rose could almost feel herself go weak in the knees.

The loud knocking came again.

"*Please,*" *Rose wasn't above begging at this point. "Just make yourself not visible or whatever it is you do." She hustled out to the foyer. It sounded as if James would break the door down any minute.*

Wrenching it open, she stepped back as James's hand swept forward, mid-arc to pound again.

"James, what are you doing here?"

"What do you mean, what am I doing here? The better question is why are you here?" He pushed passed her and into the apartment. "You made me look like a fool Rose. No sooner had I announced our engagement and you were nowhere to be seen."

"I told you I wasn't feeling well." Rose crossed her arms over her chest and glared at him. "And, if you remember correctly, I never agreed to marry you. You shouldn't have put me in that position."

"Oh, come on Rose. We both know you were going to say yes. You like this apartment, don't you? You like the way other women get jealous when they see you with me. You like having nice things and fancy clothes. And I know you like me."

He stepped forward and pulled her closer. She tried to step back, but his arms were a vice around her waist. His breath carried the unmistakable aroma of one too many bourbons. Before she could stop him, James brought his mouth down on hers and kissed her. It was a kiss full of violent passion—greedy and wild. Rose struggled to push him back. She forced her lips shut and turned her face, grimacing against the feel of his tongue on her skin.

"What is wrong with you?" he barked. "You've never been like this before."

He looked at her with such disdain as he shook his head and loosened his tie. In the world her wish and the djinn's magic created, Rose must have welcomed his advances. Now she wanted nothing more than to unwish the whole thing.

"I think you should leave James." She used the back of her hand to scrub at her lips. The only saving grace was knowing she could undo all this tomorrow. She just had to make it until then.

"Fuck that, Rose. I'm staying. We need to work this out. I'll not have you sending me away like some lovesick idiot." He pulled his tie off and toed off his expensive shoes. Making his way to the kitchen, he grabbed a glass and pulled a bottle of gin from the cabinet. "Is this all you have? I thought I told you to order in some bourbon for when I'm over."

Rose wasn't sure what to do. She wanted him gone, but short of calling the police, she had no idea how to make him go.

James was heading toward her bedroom, the glass of gin halfway to his mouth when he stopped cold.

"I do believe, Rose has asked you to leave."

Rose's stomach dropped. Oh no, no, no. The djinn stood in her doorway, arms crossed over his naked chest, aquamarine eye blazing unnaturally.

He was quite possibly the most attractive man she had ever seen but this was not the time to dwell on that little tidbit.

"Who. The hell. Are you?" James looked as if he might kill the djinn. "And why the fuck are you in my apartment?"

"I thought this was Rose's apartment. My mistake." The djinn smirked—actually smirked—at James before winking at her again.

Rose, sensing James was about to do something rash, rushed over and put a placating hand on his arm. "James. I can explain." But could she? Not really? What could she say? Sorry James, in reality, I despise everything about you, but this man is a djinn and he has magically made you think we're in love so that I can live in this posh apartment? No, that most certainly would not do her any favors.

In the end, it didn't matter. James had no interest in hearing her explanations. He turned violently toward her, the glass in his hand flying as he pushed her off him. Rose stumbled back, tripping over her own feet. "So, this is why you left the party? You could have just told me you were screwing someone, Rose. It would have saved us a lot of embarrassment."

"Oh," the djinn said. "We aren't screwing." Yet, his expression read. James lost his composure completely at the implied but unspoken word. He flew at the djinn, a drunken rage fueled mess of uninterpretable curses and wildly swinging fists. The djinn looked amused with the entire thing, stepping easily out of the way and doing nothing to defend himself. Try as he might, James couldn't land a single blow and soon his energy was spent right alongside his dignity.

"I want you out of this apartment by the end of the day tomorrow." He spat the words at Rose as he gathered up his things. "And don't bother showing up at the bank. I'll have someone collect your things."

Rose didn't argue. She knew she and the djinn would sort everything the following day. In truth, she was just happy to see him go. She followed him toward the door, ready to lock it again after he departed.

James scooped up his shoes and tie and had almost made it to the door when his eyes fell on the vase.

In one final act of violent spite, he picked up the metal vessel and pitched it as hard as he could toward the djinn. The silver object flew end over end directly toward the copper haired man's face. At the last second, the djinn grabbed the vase with blinding speed. The moment his skin made contact with the vessel, a cloud of cinnamon scented periwinkle smoke erupted from the lip of the container.

It filled the room and by the time it cleared, the metallic vase was resting on the ground, its shine dulled once more. Rose was alone. Both James and the djinn had disappeared.

Doria's phone erupted with the smoky voice of Stevie Nicks. *Stop Draggin' My Heart Around* had long been one of her favorite songs, but it might be time to change the ringtone. Its disruption had her sighing her frustration. The rocking melody meant it was time for her to get ready for work. She briefly considered calling out but she'd never failed to show for a shift at the café.

She rushed through brushing her teeth and pulling up her hair before throwing on jeans and a clean tank.

Looking at the clock, she gave herself ten minutes to speed-read through the rest of the story.

Rose didn't sleep for the rest of the night.

She didn't know if James had gone of his own volition, or if the djinn and his dramatic display had something to do with it.

The following day, she expected her rotary phone to ring, James on the other end, demanding she vacate the apartment. She would have packed up her things, but none of the clothing in the closet had been hers before the wish, and she didn't feel as if she should take it with her. At any moment, the doorman from downstairs was likely to appear, ready to escort her out.

When noon came and went with no sign of her imminent eviction or the mysterious djinn, she began to worry about a whole other set of problems. What if the djinn wasn't coming back? Worse, what if wherever he'd gone, he'd taken James with him? She wouldn't miss him, but she didn't like the idea of being implicated in his disappearance.

Deciding she needed to do something, she grabbed the djinn's vessel and began scrubbing at it vigorously.

Within no time, the metal grew warm to her touch and the gleaming shine returned.

As with the previous day, cinnamon scented smoke poured out. Rose held her breath waiting.

As the djinn stepped out of the smoke, a wave of relief washed through her. Without thinking, she raced forward and threw her arms around his waist, hugging him tightly.

"You came back," she breathed into his crisp white shirt.

"It does appear that way."

"I'm so sorry. I should have thought to try to release you sooner. I don't know what I was thinking."

He didn't answer and Rose realized he probably didn't want her hanging all over him. She stepped back quickly, ready to apologize again, but when she saw the deep frown on his face, she hesitated.

"You have nothing to apologize for," he said. "It is the way things are. If I'm not too close to the prison, I can generally resist its pull. I shouldn't have touched it."

"I don't think you had much choice," Rose argued. "James Montgomery doesn't like to be made a fool of. I just wish you'd stayed hidden last night like I asked."

"I wasn't about to hide and cower when he was treating you that way. And I should be the one apologizing to you. I never should have fulfilled your wish in such a manner." He looked genuinely distraught over it.

"Well then, let's get to fixing that shall we?" Rose said.

"It's not yet time. We have a few hours before the magic has reset."

"So then what do we do?" she asked.

"I take it you aren't moving out?" He looked around.

"Well, no. I mean, I'm not sure where I would go. Is my old apartment even still my old apartment?"

He pursed his lips and shook his head. "Probably not."

"Then I guess we're staying here. Unless James shows up, that is." Rose looked nervously about. "You didn't make him go somewhere last night, did you?"

He laughed. "No. Why?"

"He was gone when the smoke cleared. Just like you were."

The djinn scoffed. "Probably realized it was better to go than to make an even bigger ass of himself." He got a thoughtful look on his face as if he was deciding what to say next. Or more likely, how to say it. "Cadogan." He looked at her expectantly after the word left his lips.

"I'm sorry," she grimaced.

"Cadogen. It's my name."

She smiled widely. "Very nice to meet you Cadogen."

"Thank you for releasing me. Today, I mean. You could have left me in there for all the trouble I've caused."

"I would never." She looked aghast. "Besides, you had no way to know. About James that is."

He nodded once.

"So," Rose said. "Looks like we've got some time to kill."

Rose made a small roasted chicken with fluffy potatoes and a healthy side of mixed peas and carrots. She was pleased to see djinns weren't opposed to good old-fashioned American cooking. Cadogen talked more than she expected, and while he didn't exactly reveal the secrets of the universe to her, she did get quite a lesson in magical etiquette, history, and the physics of stuffing such a spectacular body into the cramped confines of the vase-like vessel he called his prison.

"But you didn't do anything wrong?" she asked.

"How do you mean?" he asked around a mouthful of potatoes.

"You call it a prison. Is it a sentence for crimes committed?"

"No. At least not that I can recall. My earliest memory is of being in there." His face shuttered at the recollection. "But you must know, not everyone who is held against their will has done something to warrant it."

She agreed and they finished their meal in companionable silence.

When the dishes were done and the sun had faded from the sky, Cadogen told her it was time for her to make her wish.

When she hesitated, he studied her closely. "What's wrong?"

"I'm nervous." She chewed her lower lip. "What if I don't word it correctly? I can't just say put it back the way it was, can I? I don't want to make things worse."

"You could say that, but I get the sense you don't want to completely waste the wish, correct?"

"I suppose not. What do I say?" she looked up at him with pleading eyes.

"Ah, Rose. I can't tell you what to wish for. If I could," he clasped her hands, "life would be so much simpler."

"For you or for me?" she teased.

"For everyone."

She took a steadying breath. "Right. So, I don't want to be attached to James Montgomery anymore and I'm not asking for love I didn't earn. I don't want to be penniless and I don't want success that isn't my own. I want James to forget he saw you, but I don't want to forget you. Is that too much to ask for?"

"No. I don't think it is. But remember, I'm only the conduit for the magic. I can try to sway it, but I can't make any promises." He looked at her gravely. So different from the night before when the entire thing had seemed like little

more than a joke to him. "Do you understand? The magic can be-"

"Tricky," she said at the same time as the djinn.

He smiled. "Right. Here we go. Say the words and I shall serve your wish."

"I'd like for you to grant my wish as I spoke it."

He crossed his arms, but before he could continue, she blurted out, "Please."

The djinn smiled and his head came down in a nod.

Rose blinked and she was back in her old apartment. It was still evening and she could feel the breeze blowing in through the open window of her bedroom.

She hopped out of bed where she'd been lying, and realized she was clad only in a thin night dress.

Music floated in from the small living space and the deep baritone of a man humming along drew her up short.

What had Cadogen done now?

"Hello," she called.

The humming stopped. "Out here, love."

Love? The voice was familiar, but it had certainly not called her love before.

She crept forward and peeked out the door. Standing in the kitchen, his back to her, was Cadogen. His copper hair was tousled and the bronzed skin of his once again shirtless back was slightly flushed. The alluring scent of warm sweet bread filled the air. He was busy mixing something in a bowl.

Curiosity got the better of her and she approached to look over his shoulder. Her griddle was filled with fluffy pancakes. "You're making breakfast. At night?"

"I wanted something sweet, but this was all I could think of," he said. He continued stirring the remaining batter as he bent down and placed a quick kiss on the tip of her

nose. Rose surprised herself by not jumping back. In fact, she leaned in closer and snuggled against his side.

It was odd. She knew she had only just met him but the act seemed like one of long practiced affection. It didn't have the same oily feel of her wish-based relationship with James Montgomery.

"Hmm." He smirked as he looked at her. "I kind of like that."

"I kind of like it too," she said honestly. "But . . ."

"You want to know if I've magicked you into something?"

"The thought had crossed my mind, yes."

"The answer is I have no idea."

"That's a little scary. I did say I wasn't wishing for love. I made it quite clear."

"You did. I know. I specifically focused on the important things. Getting rid of James, making sure you weren't penniless, and remembering me." He smiled. "And here we are."

"Here we are."

Rose and Cadogen ate their pancakes smothered in syrup. They sat up late continuing their earlier conversation about all things magic. Rose told him about her life in the city, the family she lost when she was just out of high school, her friends, and her dreams. Talking about her friends, she ran to the phone and dialed Gert's number. Her friend seemed bemused by the late-night contact and Rose's insistence that she promised they were still friends.

Eventually, it was time for bed. Rose felt awkward that she didn't feel awkward inviting Cadogen to lie down with her.

After turning out the light, Cadogen pulled her close to his warm body. Rose turned her face up to him. She ran her fingers over his lips and through his hair. He kissed her gently at first, but within minutes, the gentleness turned to hunger. It was nothing like the violent kiss she endured from James. It was raw and beseeching and utterly wonderful.

"Is this real?" she whispered the words against his lips and the djinn stilled. Rose immediately regretted voicing the words aloud.

"I don't mean for you to stop," she explained. "It just seems too perfect. You are too perfect."

"I'm the furthest thing from perfect you can imagine." Cadogen rolled off her and stared at the ceiling. "The things I've done. The wishes I've put into being. Not everyone is like you Rose. Some people request the most profoundly horrible things. And though I may not like it, I am bound to grant them."

"I can't imagine what it's like for you."

"Nor should you want to." He closed his eyes and the pain she felt radiating off him was so acute, it felt as if her own heart would break on his account.

"What will happen after my last wish?" Her voice was small, and though she dreaded the answer, she needed to know.

"I will return to my prison and you will have what it is you wished for." His voice was flat.

"Well then, I'll just rub the lamp again and you'll return." She said it matter-of-factly.

"It doesn't work that way. After the wish is granted, the vessel will no longer be in your possession. It'll turn up somewhere, sometime, of its choosing. For someone else."

Rose sat up straight and peered down at him. "No."

"There is no 'No' Rose. The magic does as it wills."

"And if I never make a third wish?" She asked.

He sighed loudly. "It'll work for a time, but eventually, you'll have to. It's just the way things are done."

"Last night you told me you had to return to the vase unless certain steps are taken. What are the steps,

Cadogen?" Her voice was tinged with something close to anger.

"I can't tell you, Rose. I wish," he smirked at her, "I could, but I can't. Come here." He motioned for her to lie down in the cradle of his arms and she obliged. "Let's just get some sleep and perhaps things will look better in the morning."

Rose didn't want to argue so she did as he asked. Laying with her head on his shoulder and a leg thrown over his hips, she finally drifted off to sleep.

Rose was true to her word. She didn't so much as ask Cadogen to grant her anything over the next several weeks. She didn't ask him to hold the door, though he held each and every one they encountered. She didn't ask him to do the dishes, though he always shared clean-up duty with her at night after dinner. She didn't ask him to pay her rent, or purchase their groceries, or splurge on tickets to a matinee movie. She didn't even ask him to tell her he loved her. He hadn't said the words and she promised him she would never demand it of him. She felt her love for him growing each day, but she kept the truth of that to herself.

Rose went to work each day, where she avoided her boss Mr. Montgomery at every turn. He still made a point of standing too close and brushing against her in the elevator too often. And every now and then she'd catch him looking at her with a strange look in his eye, as if something about her struck some memory he couldn't quite place.

She continued to lunch with Gertrude when they had the chance and she continued to greet the customers at the bank like old friends or family. She did her job and did it well, but as each day went by, she felt as if a sword were hanging over her head. She knew eventually, it would all come crashing down.

Cadogen didn't belong here. The magic or the universe or the mystery that possessed him—the thing that made him djinn— didn't fancy him living outside the bonds of his prison. She knew it in her bones.

Someday, the magic would have its way and he'd be ripped from her. She didn't think she'd be able to pull herself together when it did.

It was on the bus ride home one night when she was feeling this most acutely that a terrible awful idea occurred to her. What if she were to wish they had never met? Was such a thing possible? She didn't want to ask him for fear it would break his heart as surely as the idea broke hers. But if she could make the wish for neither of them to remember, it might work. He would grant it and the slate would be wiped clean. She would go back to her solitary lonely life, and he would go back to his vessel. Neither would have any memory of the love they'd shared or the treachery of her breaking it off.

But then he'd be trapped in his prison. Even if she didn't remember it later, knowing she'd sentenced him to such a thing was unthinkable.

There had to be another way.

Still, she sensed their time together was short.

That night Rose made love to Cadogen as if it might be their last time together. She gave herself to him completely. Slowly at first and then with a wild abandon, she'd never let herself experience. Her want for him was insatiable. She worshiped him with her mouth and her soul. Her body and her heart. She let him take her over the edge twice before she returned the favor on her knees before him.

Afterward, she lay at his side and studied every plane and angle of his face. She focused on his copper hair and brilliant bright eyes and tried to memorize every detail of his skin. *Each ridge of his muscle. The exact feel of him inside her.*

She was determined to keep the tears at bay, not willing to ruin what might be her last moments with him. She'd tried to convince herself not to wish him away, but how long would it be before she was forced to act?

"You feel it too," he said softly.

She could only nod against him, afraid if she spoke, the tears would indeed come.

"I will cherish each memory of our time together. These weeks will sustain me for the decades and centuries to come. I'll never forget you, Rose."

It was that statement alone that made her realize she would never go through with such a horrific wish. He'd said some people wished for terrible things. This had to be the worst wish of all.

The tears were burning behind her eyes and her throat felt thick. She couldn't breathe with the unfairness of it all. She'd finally found someone who made her happy. Even if his magic had played some small role in it, she felt she'd earned his love just as he'd earned hers.

"Ah, love. Tell me what you're thinking." *He whispered the words into her hair.*

"I don't know. I just wish this wasn't happening. I wish I wasn't going to lose you. I wish you weren't leaving me. I wish that damn vase was just a vase and not your prison." *The words came hard and fast without her realizing what it was she was saying.*

His breath stilled. "What else do you wish." *His voice was barely above a whisper but filled with such urgency she finally realized what she was saying. How important it was.*

Sitting up, she scrubbed the tears from her eyes and looked at him. It couldn't possibly be that easy, could it?

Certainly, no. In all the centuries of his existence, had no one ever dared to wish him free?

"Tell me, Rose. What else do you wish?" He'd sat up too and was holding her hands to his bare chest.

She said the words slowly, a question in each one as they passed her lips. "I wish you weren't a djinn?" He nodded encouragingly.

"That you were a mortal man who loved me? That you want to stay here with me too?"

He crushed her to him. "Yes, Rose. Yes. That is the most perfect of wishes."

"But I don't want to wish for your love. I promised I wouldn't do that."

"You can't wish for something you already have." He held her face in his hands and kissed her sweetly. "I've loved you for quite some time now."

"And it will work?" Her hope was a crushing thing. If it failed, she might never recover.

"I believe it will. You just have to ask. And be careful. The magic can be—"

"Tricky. Yes, I know." She continued to hold on to him as if the djinn were a lifeline and she was lost at sea. "I would like you to serve me my final wish. I wish for you to stay with me, here Cadogen. No longer a djinn and no longer imprisoned. I wish for you to stay here and continue to love me and let me love you. I wish for the only magic that you must serve to be that which we make together. I won't bother to ask for eternity with you. I know that isn't allowed."

Cadogen raised her hands to his lips and kissed them. Then he let them fall. He grinned broadly as he crossed his arms over his chest and nodded.

9

DORIA practically danced her way to work.

Banking on Fortune had to be the story to set Miles free. It had to be.

A magical genie—or in this case djinn—trapped in a terrible prison, only to be set free by the woman who loved him. This had to be the story.

"*. . . not everyone who is held against their will has done something to warrant it.*"

If this wasn't the one, she had no idea where else to go. One way or another, she would find out that night.

During her breaks, she read through the book again and again. After five full repeats, she felt she knew the story well enough to recite it to Miles, should the book not make it back into dreamland with her. She couldn't wait to see the look on his face when the words worked their magic and the spell was broken, leaving Miles to walk in the world once again.

10

IT HADN'T worked.

The fucking story hadn't worked and Miles' blossom of hope had been crushed and Doria was in shock and the fucking story hadn't worked.

Doria was still reeling. She had been so sure. So, so, sure.

She couldn't even blame it on getting the words wrong, as the book had in fact been waiting for her in Vespertine Books when she'd fallen asleep and dreamed herself into Miles' arms. She'd fallen all over herself telling him about the book and how she was going to break the curse. He'd been so excited to hear her read it to him. She'd sat in her favorite chair and he placed himself on the sofa to listen to her recite from the pages. She snapped it shut on the last words with a triumphant grin and then they'd waited.

And waited.

And waited.

There was no feeling of magic, no firing dissolution of the bonds around them. They were still just Doria and Miles. Sitting in Doria's dream in the dimly lit space that was both Vespertine Books and Miles' prison.

In Doria's dream.

"Maybe it's because this is in my head," Dorai mused.

"We've discussed this. It's not just your head. It's mine too."

"Yes, I know, but maybe the curse wasn't broken because we aren't actually in the bookshop. We're both dreaming. Maybe I need to tell you the story in the real waking world."

"That's all well and good, but if you can't find it, you can't find it."

Peter's curse must have known its time was coming to an end. There was no other reason for it to suddenly be so difficult to find.

The dream began to grow watery and thin. She was waking, and try as she might, Doria couldn't force herself to stay asleep.

"I'm not giving up Miles."

She woke with a start and immediately began to cry.

Days continued to tick by and the temperatures began to cool. Each morning was another exercise in frustration as Doria would wake to another day without Miles in the flesh. The leaves showed only the barest traces of warm colors and the full autumn riot of oranges and reds was still several weeks off. Despite this, pumpkins began appearing on porches and ghosts appeared in neighborhood trees.

"When is the anniversary night exactly?" Doria asked Cassie over a cup of tea on the library steps.

"Next Tuesday, the twenty-first." Cassie blew over the small hole in the plastic lid of her cup. "We usually plan to meet him in the park. It's the one place that never seems to change. No matter where the bookshop door opens, he can get there easily."

Doria nodded. "Makes sense. I'll double check with him tonight and make sure he's still on the same page."

Cassie sat quietly, but Doria could sense she wanted to say something.

"What is it?"

"Well, it's just. . . I don't want you to get your hopes up." Her short pixie hair ruffled in the breeze.

"You've all said it's his one night of freedom." A small line appeared between Doria's brows.

"It is," Cassie agreed.

"Then why wouldn't he show?"

"Think about it," Cassie said not unkindly. "Nothing has been typical for the last few months. We've never gone this long without having access to the shop. It's all too possible whatever magic Peter is using to keep him in that place, he won't allow it to slip for the night as he typically does."

Doria's heart stilled. She hadn't thought about it. She'd just blindly assumed this year would be no different as far as the magic went, but really how ridiculous was that? Nothing about this entire thing was typical.

She couldn't allow the idea to take root. Miles had to have his one night of freedom. If he didn't, her last-ditch plan was sure to fail.

Doria didn't share Cassondra's concerns with Miles, but even without discussing it, she could tell he had the same concerns. He was distracted and tense each time she dreamt of him.

On Sunday evening, she finally worked up the nerve to mention the anniversary.

"How exactly has it worked in the past?"

"As far as the magic goes, I have no idea, but essentially, on midnight early Tuesday morning, I'll just be able to walk out the door and find myself in town somewhere. I get twenty-four hours, and no matter where I am or what I'm doing when that moment hits, I blink and I'm back here. The first year was the worst. I thought the curse was broken and I was sleeping on the sofa at my brother's house-- that's Elenor's dad-- with William in my arms. It was bliss like I'd never experienced. The next thing I knew, I was back in the shop. I'd never been brought so low in all my life. Made quite the mess of the place."

Doria rubbed her hands through his hair as he reclined into her. She'd soothe away all his hurt if she could.

"We made a note of the date and the following year I was a bit more prepared. Each year after it was the same. Eventually, I just started coming back to the shop when I knew midnight was drawing close. It seemed easier in a sense."

"You know people think you're a ghost don't you?" Doria tried to lighten the mood.

"I've heard."

"Has the door ever not been here when you go back?"

"Nope. Not once. It's always in the same place I left it."

Doria nodded.

"I want to try to come back with you." Her voice was little more than a whisper.

"What? No." He sat up away from her. "I can't let you do that. What if you get stuck?"

"Would it be so bad?"

"Yes, Doria. It would. Oh, don't look at me like that. You know that's not what I meant." His voice wasn't angry but it was firm. "I absolutely will not let you give your life away like that."

"It wouldn't be giving my life away. Look, Miles. I don't have a great life out there and if being stuck here with you means I get to be with you, I'd take that any day. A thousand times."

"Doria."

"No. Let me finish. I would take that and so much more, but if it makes you feel any better, I don't think I'd be stuck. Just because the shop doesn't want to let me in, does not mean it won't be happy to let me go." She honestly had no idea what the shop would or wouldn't do, but that wasn't the point. She had a plan. Not one she was ready to share with Miles just yet, but a plan just the same.

The air was brisk and cool. It smelled of newly lit chimneys laced with newly fallen leaves.

Elenor was bundled up and sandwiched between Cassondra and Felicity. Doria's roommate had proclaimed there was no chance of missing out on meeting Miles and had packed two large thermoses full of warm apple cider for the wait. She was doing her best to force a mug of it on Doria.

Unlike the other women, Doria was having trouble sitting on the park bench in the dead of night. The place was deserted and frankly, more than a little creepy. She paced back and forth, trying and failing to calm her nerves. More than once, she swore she saw Peter Smith lurking in the shadows, but each time she peered closer, she'd find nothing more interesting than a trashcan or toppled tree.

She must have checked her watch a dozen times between when they arrived promptly at 11:45 and when Miles finally rushed through the gate at 12:09.

He wasn't dressed for the weather.

It was a ridiculous thing to notice, but Doria did.

And then she was running to him.

She stopped just short, not wanting to tackle him and still just the slightest bit concerned that all of the dreams of him from the past three months had been just that. Dreams. Her mind's way of filling in the blank space her heart needed Miles to fill.

One corner of his mouth ticked up and light filled his eyes. "I would have thought after last night's festivities you'd be happier to see me. Or was I not as good as I thought I was?"

Doria's brain flashed back to him taking her over the back of a chair just before she'd woken that morning and color flushed her cheeks.

"It was real." She smiled. "All of it was real?"

He bit at his lower lip as he grinned and nodded. It was the grin that undid her. She flung herself forward and wrapped her arms around his neck drawing him down so she could feast on his mouth.

She'd never once complained about her time dreaming of Miles and his lips and arms, teeth and body, but having him in the flesh was infinitely better. Heat crashed through her and she savored each stroke of his tongue. Each nibble of his teeth. Each sweep of his lips.

"You two might want to save up some of that energy. You've got a whole day to suck the lungs from one another." Elenor toddled up and patted Miles on the shoulder, forcing him to draw back from Doria and turn to embrace his niece. She wiped a tear from her cheek as he let her go and then crushed Cassie to him in an equally ferocious hug.

"We missed you too," she said as he released her.

"Felicity?" He asked as he noticed Doria's roommate standing to the side.

"That's me." She rocked up on her tiptoes a giddy smile on her face. "I've been dying to meet you, Miles."

He moved to shake her hand, but Felicity was having none of it. She threw her arms around him and squeezed just as the other woman had. He laughed and hugged her back.

"Let's head to my place." Elenor was already heading toward the park gate. "I've got a great pot of chowder on the stove. We could all do with a bit of warming up."

Cassie stopped up beside her and extended her arms for Elenor to balance on and Felicity trotted to her other side. Whether to help, or simply give Doria and Miles a bit of distance, Doria didn't know. Grabbing Miles' hand, she laced her fingers through his, leaned into his shoulder, and followed them out of the park.

The chowder was delicious and the company divine. Doria marveled at how at ease Miles was despite knowing he was there on borrowed time. She wondered too if William's passing put it all into perspective or if he just hid his grief well.

Not wanting to get their hopes up yet again, she hadn't discussed her plan to take one more stab at freeing him with the others.

After several hours of chatting, the dawn's peachy light began to diffuse through Elenor's home. Felicity said her goodbyes and told Doria with a wink she was headed to Mik's place.

"I'll be back tonight." Miles gave Elenor and Cassie each a quick peck on the cheek.

Doria led him through the quiet streets to her apartment, lost in watching him savor each passing breeze, stray cat, and early morning vehicle they passed.

"Can't believe I finally get to see where you live."

"Prepare to be exceedingly unimpressed." She unlocked the door and stood back as he stepped inside. She watched as he took in the cramped apartment, a slow smile transforming his already handsome face. "I love it. It's all so. . .you."

He turned and grabbed her by the hips, pulling her closer until their bodies aligned. He ran his fingertips over her lips and she shivered.

"I don't want to go back." His forehead tilted forward until it rested against hers.

"I know." She ran her hands up the back of his neck and into his hair. "Are you tired?"

"I'm more awake right now than I've been in a very long time, Doria."

She bit at her bottom lip. "Good. I don't want to sleep and miss a moment of you."

He cupped her face and used his thumbs to stroke her cheeks. "Not a moment," he agreed before he captured her lips with a moan.

Doria's body reacted immediately. The feel of him in her arms. The softness of his skin. The smell of books and cedar lingering in his hair. The taste of him on her tongue. It was a heady mix that stole her heart and sent her flesh into the sweetest frenzy.

Without breaking the kiss, she began to walk him backward toward her tiny bedroom. When they reached the edge of the mattress, she pushed him down into the warmth of her comforter with one hand before adjusting the lights and starting up a relaxing playlist on her phone with the other.

"All the new technology," he shook his head. "I never would have believed such things would exist. Straight out of Orwell or Bradbury."

"Mmm-hmm." She dropped down on top of him and took her time kissing her way from his mouth to the tip of his toes, undressing him as she went.

He was here. With her. In the flesh. And his flesh was delicious to behold.

They spent the better part of the day tangled in each other's limbs, but as the afternoon drew toward evening, Doria began to feel not only anxious but also selfish. She had every intention of doing her best to free him later, but if she failed, she didn't want him to miss out on a moment of his precious time.

"Isn't there anywhere else you'd like to go? Anyone else you'd like to see?" She asked into his chest where she was curled up.

"I need to stop by Elenor's on the way back. And I'd like to visit the cemetery as well."

The cemetery? Of course, he'd want to see William's gravestone. She hadn't even considered it before. She was a selfish bitch.

"Of course. I'm sorry I didn't think about that earlier." She scrambled off the bed and pulled on her jeans and sweater.

"You have nothing to be sorry for." He pulled her hand to his lips and kissed the inside of her wrist before hauling himself out of bed.

They stopped at the small graveyard and Doria wandered between the stones reading dates stretching back over one hundred and fifty years. She didn't want to intrude on Miles as he stood over the marker of the son who'd lived into his eighties.

As she walked around one of several above-ground mausoleums, she caught movement off to her right. There, by the entrance to the cemetery, was none other than Peter Smith. The way he watched Miles made her skin crawl, but she'd be damned if she was going to go chasing after the man again. He could stand and watch all night if he wanted. Turning her back on him, she made her way back to Miles and the pair left just as the last blushes of light left the sky.

After two more emotional stops—Elenor's and Cassondra's—Miles led Doria back past the park and down the street to the small alcove where she'd always entered the bookshop before.

And there it was. Despite the number of times the graffiti tagged brick wall between the appliance store and the clothing consignment had been just that, a brick wall, as they approached Doria saw the worn wooden sign and the glass-paneled door leading into the magically cursed space. She glanced at her watch. 11:52. They only had minutes to get inside if she was going with Miles. After midnight, the way might very well disappear.

"I still don't like this," Miles said as his hand closed on the brass knob.

"I understand that, but I'm afraid you're still stuck with me." Doria lifted to her tiptoes and planted a kiss on his cheek. "Let's go."

He was turning the knob when dark smudges along the doorframe caught Doria's eyes. As she watched they grew and thickened, transforming from simple smoke stains to charcoal burns and twisted wood. Great flakes of ash settled and drifted to the ground even as heat emanated from the brick. Miles followed her gaze and tugged her hand.

"Times almost up." His voice was broken.

"Having a party are we?" The flesh on the back of Doria's neck crawled and her heart sank as she recognized the sound of Peter's voice from several feet behind her.

She didn't know exactly how the curse had worked, or what dark magic the weasel possessed, but Doria absolutely knew, she did not want the man inside Vespertine Books with them when she tried once again to break it.

"Go." She pushed Miles forward and stepped inside behind him, slamming the door shut on Peter's face.

11

"**you** bitch!"

Peter had managed to wedge his hand between the door and the jam. It must have hurt like hell, but still, he didn't relent.

"Let me in, Miles." He'd pushed his face up to the crack and the manic look in the one eye Doria could see told her everything she needed to know. He wasn't happy she was here and under no circumstance could she allow him inside before she was done.

"Sorry!" Doria called as she pushed her weight into the door. "Shop's closed." She'd snap his fingers off if needed.

Miles stood shoulder to shoulder with her. "Let up just a bit." He whispered the words into the shell of her ear.

Doria did as he asked and as soon as she did, Peter withdrew his hand and pushed harder into the door. Thankfully, he was no match for the combined weight of Miles and Doria. With one final push, the door clicked shut and Peter howled in outrage.

Miles slammed the lock shut.

Up until that moment, Doria hadn't even realized the shop could be locked. She'd just assumed if the door could be found, it could be opened. There was still so much she didn't understand, but hopefully, she wouldn't need those answers in the future.

"Will that keep him out?" She stared at the door as pounding sounded from the other side.

Miles ran a hand through his hair. "It should. I went through a period about a decade ago when I kept the door locked all the time.

My family had a secret little knock and I'd only open up if it was one of them. The lock kept everyone else out. Including Peter."

Doria thought of her first day in the shop and how she'd mistaken Peter for Miles. The thought of how wrong she'd been burned like acid in her stomach. "Does he show up often?"

"Now and again. He likes to pop in and *check up* on me."

Doria cocked her head and closed her eyes, willing her anger to subside at all the injustice Miles had suffered over the years. Part of her wondered, even if her plan worked, would he ever be able to adjust to life outside the beautiful shop or would he be lost in the world out there? Even worse, a possibility she barely let herself consider, if the curse lifted, would all of the time come crashing back? Would Miles age seventy-five years when the magic finally freed him?

As horrible as the idea was, she knew he'd take that over being stuck in the terrible purgatory he'd been subjected to.

She grabbed his hands and pulled him over to the reading sofa. "I have an idea I want to try."

He quirked an eyebrow. "I thought you might be all worn out."

"Not that kind of an idea." She smiled as he got comfortable on the sofa. "I want to tell you a story."

"A story?" He leaned forward and rested his elbows on his knees. "That's why you wanted to come with me tonight. To tell me one in person?"

She nodded.

"Did you find another book somewhere?"

"No." Her pulse was starting to pound as she sensed his skepticism.

He sighed. "I don't want you to get your hopes up, Doria. I know you want this as much as I do, but. . . "

"Just let me try. It isn't the same as last time. I'm not going to read to you." She nodded and bit her lip. "I'm going to give you a story I've written in my head. I know it might sound a little ridiculous, but I think it's worth a shot."

"*Doria.*" It was the saddest she'd ever seen him look and it broke her. He'd always been so full of light, *so full of life*. To see him now, ripped her heart in two.

Well fuck that. He could be sad later. If it didn't work. She wasn't going to give up before she at least tried one more time.

"Listen to me, Miles. We are going to do this. End of discussion."

He held up his hands in surrender. "I can't fight with you. Not when you're here. I. . . " He hung his head and then snapped out of it and sat upright. He didn't smile but she could see he was willing to let her do what she wanted.

"Okay. That's better." She tried to smile, but it was forced. "No fire or steal or penned prose shall end the bond, but if words of merit are born from hate, only then will time be restored," she recited from memory. "Do you see? *Penned prose. No penned prose.* It can't be me just reading you a story. I have to tell you one that comes from me."

He shook his head and sighed. "Let's give it a shot."

A loud bang came from the front door. Peter *really* wanted to come inside. *Tough shit.*

She nodded briskly and took a deep breath.

"Once upon a time, there was a dashing king who lived in a palace built of words and stories rather than bricks and mortar. Where other palaces had buttresses and beams, this king's palace had ink and paper. In place of wood and glass, his palace had leather and canvas, glue and bindings, spines and parchment." She looked at him from under her lashes, suddenly quite self-conscious.

"It's good. Keep Going."

"It might be easier if I sit over there, so I don't have to watch you watch me."

He patted the spot on the sofa next to him and she switched spots, nestling into the space under his arm.

"In each nook and cranny of the palace, stories lived. The dashing king was the keeper of them all. Plots were his servants, themes and tropes his court.

"Some of the pages told stories bold and daring others sweet yet intoxicating. Others still clever. Even more, dull or captivating. The monarch, like any just ruler, took care of them all, and while he had his favorites, each book and volume were treated as if it alone ruled his heart."

Doria paused as Peter's assault on the front door increased in both tempo and magnitude.

Miles squeezed her shoulder and she took a deep breath before continuing.

"One day, while the young king was holding court, a dark wizard arrived and asked the king to kill a portion of his court and destroy a wing of his castle. The sorcerer argued these stories were too daring, too insightful, and too wonderful to be allowed to stay with the others. They would lead others astray he claimed. Only stories the sorcerer favored should be allowed to remain."

Miles began rubbing small circles on Doria's arm, his movements a metronome for her words.

"The king was appalled by this notion and told the sorcerer as much, but the evil wizard laughed at the king calling him a weak ruler. The dark wizard offered to rule in his place, but only if the monarch would also banish the one person the king loved most in the world, his young son and heir to his throne."

Miles' hand stilled. "Oh," he breathed. "Am I the king?

Doria hushed him and continued.

"As the king loved the books equally—and the tiny prince even more—he refused and exiled the sorcerer from his realm, asking him to leave and never return. This of course angered the evil man and in a fit of rage, he set fire to the palace and all within its walls.

"Unable to flee the burning embers, the dashing king was trapped in the palace.

"Thankfully, the young prince had been away from the castle on an adventure the day of the conflagration and was spared from the flames. The stories too, survived. They had a will of their own and could not be contained."

Peter's banging turned to a nauseating screech and Doria wondered if the wood and metal of the door frame would buckle under the weight of the noise alone.

"Should I," she tried to stand, unsure what to do. If he broke down the door, she wasn't sure she could finish the story.

Miles' eyes flashed to the entrance. "Keep going."

"What happened next confused and surprised not only the king but the wizard as well. The wizard and the king were chained by the curse—bound to the palace of stories as well as each other. For generations, they circled one another. The sorcerer seeking vengeance for his own failed magic and the king seeking solace in his prison.

"For many lifetimes, the two were locked in silent battle, trapped within the walls of the palace with only the haunting words to keep them company. But while the evil sorcerer grew in his fear of the haunts in the halls, the king welcomed the chance to become acquainted with each of his subjects. As time ceased to spin, he read every word, studied every picture, and cared for each scrap of ink and paper in his care. The sorcerer was driven mad with his hatred of everything the king stood for, but try as he might he could not break the king of his spirit."

Dora stopped and sniffed the air. Smoke. There was smoke drifting in from the entrance of the shop. Had Peter lit the place on fire again in the hope of flushing them out?

Panic threatened, but if he was trying this hard to stop her, she had to keep going.

"Tales of the cursed palace circulated far and wide. Villagers whispered of dark deeds and ghastly apparitions. Only a few knew the truth of the king and his subjects and over time his story became one of folklore and legend."

The acrid scent seared her nose and water began streaming from her eyes.

"Miles, is there another way out?"

"No. Only the front." She stood but refused to stop talking even as she grew closer to the stinging cloud.

"One day word of the cursed castle reached the ears of a passing knight of the vale. She was battle-scarred and hard-hearted. Anyone in their right mind avoided the knight like the viper she was."

Miles chuffed a laugh that quickly turned into a cough.

"The knight spent her life seeking out jousts and wars. It was her only distraction from her own dark pain. In hearing of the castle, she decided to challenge the haunts who called it home. Once she entered, however, she saw the still form of the king, bent over a book and tending it with care. In seeing the knight, he rose and offered her kindness and the chance to rule over the stories with him, if only she could learn to love them as he did.

"The knight was skeptical at first. No man and certainly no monarch could truly care as much as this king did. She called him a liar and called him a fraud and yet the king did not balk. He continued to offer the knight kindness." Doria drew in a ragged breath and coughed. They were just in front of the door. If she could get the last few lines out, they might have a chance. "Occasionally the knight would spy the sorcerer lurking about, but she paid him no mind. After a time, the knight realized she was in love with the king and all of his subjects. She told him as much and he smiled as if she'd given him the greatest of all treasures. This angered the evil wizard, but as the king took the knight in his arms, and vowed to make her his queen, the curse was broken and the palace was free of the curse."

She began to hack as the smoke blurred her vision and singed her lungs. They had to get out of the shop. Either the story worked or it hadn't.

Miles grew blurring in her vision. He reached for the door and yanked it open, pushing Doria out into the night. As she stumbled across the cobbled walkway, she caught sight of the flames licking up the façade of the building.

She sucked down breath after breath, turning to search for Miles. She hadn't felt him follow her out. He had to have made it though. He had to have.

Tears streamed down her face as she searched through the smoke. It looked as if the entire building was going to be engulfed soon.

Sirens wailed as rescuers headed toward the scene. Men jumped from an odd-looking red truck and began to pull hose through the streets.

Still, she searched for Miles.

After what felt like a lifetime, she saw movement in the hazy smoke. A man was stumbling under the weight of a heavy burden. It took her several long seconds to recognize Miles. He was dragging another body out. As he stumbled forward under the weight, two of the firefighters stepped up and took the lifeless form of Peter Smith from his arms.

Doria raced forward and caught Miles in her arms. She ran her hands over his face and down his arms. "Are you hurt?" She demanded.

He shook his head.

"I thought I'd lost you. I thought it didn't work." She cried into his chest as he wrapped his arms around her back.

"It worked." He tilted her face up to his and kissed her deeply. "You brilliant woman, it most certainly worked." She clung to his body like a lifeline, sure that she would never let him go. "Let me see your arm." She pulled his sleeve up and was surprised to see the scrawling ink pattern still tattooed on his skin.

"I suppose it's a little memento for me to hold on to." He shrugged.

The area outside the shop was chaos. People ran up and down the street and while something didn't set quite right with the scene, Doria couldn't put her finger on exactly what felt off. It wasn't quite as dark out as she'd remembered from earlier in the evening, but it was more than just that.

"What about Peter?" she asked Miles.

"I nearly tripped over him at the entrance. I thought he was dead, but then he started to groan and I just couldn't leave him there. After everything he'd done, I couldn't do it."

"It's because you are a good and just king," she laughed into his chest. "Do you think he'll live?"

"A good and just king who has finally found a worthy queen." He kissed the top of her head. "I don't know if he will. I guess we'll just need to wait and see."

They stood across the street—Miles focused on the fire and Doria focused on Miles. It was for that reason, neither of them noticed when a small group of people raced up to them.

The woman threw her arms around Miles and Doria stiffened. "Oh thank the lord Miles. When we saw the smoke and heard the sirens we headed down right away."

The woman was a pretty petite thing, dressed in a tea-length full skirt and matching cardigan. The man she was with looked just as shaken. He held the hand of a small boy. A girl of about ten stood next to them, wide-eyed and focused on the flames. The man used his free arm to clap Miles on the back. "You alright? You look like you've seen a ghost."

Miles did look shaken. To the core. Doria was sure it was from more than just the fire. More than just the curse.

He stared and the couple speechless. His eyes flicked between them until they fell entirely on the small boy at the man's side. He dropped to his knees and held out his arms. The toddler ran straight into them and Miles stood and spun the boy around in a wide arc as the child squealed with laughter.

Doria looked at the man and woman, still completely lost as to what was happening.

Miles turned to her, the smile on his face the most beautiful thing she'd ever seen.

"Doria, you might want to sit for a minute," he nodded toward the bench behind her. She frowned but did as he asked. She stared at him in puzzlement. Had the curse not been broken? "Miles, what's going on? Is this just another elaborate dream?"

"I don't exactly know what is going on, but I have an idea. And no, it isn't another dream. Doria," he said and he tilted his head toward the toddler. "I'd like you to meet William. My son."

Epilogue

THANKS to the very robust insurance policy Miles had on the shop, they were able to rebuild and reopen in just six months' time.

Doria loved stocking the shelves and managing the counter. Even more, she loved doing it all with Miles. She'd also come to love William in a way she had never expected. He was sunshine and light and all the things that made her want to be a better person.

Miles had told his brother and his family that he and Doria had been dating for a while, but he'd kept it quiet. Given his previous marriage, they all seemed to understand. They were married two months later in a small ceremony in the village park.

Doria had a particular fondness for Miles' niece Elenor. At just ten years old, she was a witty kid with a wicked sense of humor. Doria could spend hours with her and never grow tired of the child's presence and Elenor didn't seem to mind Doria either.

Peter Smith had indeed succumbed to his injuries, forcing Doria to accept all hope of finding a way to right her own timeline was lost as well. Whatever dark arcane magic the man possessed, died right along with him.

While Doria was happy to be wherever and whenever Miles was, there were days when she truly missed her own time. She missed the convenience technology afforded. She missed the societal changes that had occurred. She missed the vast piles of literature and the myriad of genres she'd come to love. She missed the ease with which she could obtain the said multitude of books.

Most of all, she missed Felicity.

It occurred to Doria that in this timeline, things would be different. She was looking at a future where her best friend didn't know she existed and that hurt beyond measure.

It was from this pain, in conjunction with her love of wonderful stories, she found her passion.

Miles had gifted her with a smart little typewriter ordered directly from a Sears catalog. It was the newest model but nothing compared to what she'd been used to. Nevertheless, one quiet rainy afternoon, Doria sat down and started to write.

She had the most wonderful idea for a story.

ABOUT THE AUTHOR

Aster Rye is a pen name of author Kami King Larsen. She grew up with a love for reading remarkable stories and cut her teeth on horror and sci-fi. While she still loves a good spine tingler, eventually she discovered the endless joy of fantasy and romance.

More from Aster Rye

Bittersweet Breadcrumbs

Writing as Kami King Larsen
A Simple Tale of Water and Weeping
Blood and Wonder (Medicus Corpus book 1)
Breath and Starshine (Medicus Corpus book2)

A Simple Tale of Ink and Bindings (Coming Spring of 2024)

Let's Connect
Join my mailing list for ARC books and other exciting news
www.kamikinglarsenbooks.com
Follow me on Instagram @authorkamikinglarsen
Or @lilyfernbooks
Or find me on Facebook Kami King Larsen Books and Bits

Thank you for taking the time to share in Miles and Doria's story! I'd love to know what you think! Don't forget to leave a review on Amazon, Goodreads, your social media channels, or anywhere else you review books!

www.ingramcontent.com/pod-product-compliance
Lightning Source LLC
Chambersburg PA
CBHW031541310726
48971CB00008B/2568